F.
W

Whitney, Phyllis A.
Secret of the emerald star

1652

Secret of the Emerald Star

Secret of the Emerald Star

by

PHYLLIS A. WHITNEY

Illustrated by

ALEX STEIN

THE WESTMINSTER PRESS
Philadelphia

LIBRARY OF CONGRESS CATALOG CARD No. 64–16345

PUBLISHED BY THE WESTMINSTER PRESS ®

PHILADELPHIA, PENNSYLVANIA

PRINTED IN THE UNITED STATES OF AMERICA

For Jamie Sue Brown

Who "sees" a great deal more than many sighted people I know, and whom I am proud and happy to have as my friend.

Contents

(1)

The Whirling Girl

IT WAS perfectly clear to Robin Ward that the family conference was not going well. The discussion concerned what she wanted to do more than anything else in the world, but Mother and Dad, and even her brother, Tommy, who was only nine, were arguing against her doing it. Robin felt unfairly opposed and quietly determined, all in the same breath.

The family had gathered in Robin's favorite room of the house the Wards had just moved into on Staten Island. Their home in Maywood, Illinois, outside of Chicago, was a bungalow, and there had never been enough room for the many Ward projects. This Staten Island house, built shortly after the Civil War, had more rooms than Robin had ever seen in a house. Here all sorts of things were possible.

Since getting the bookcases filled and a place arranged for reading was almost as important to the four Wards as managing to eat and sleep, they had worked hard on this room during the single week they had lived in this house. A secondhand carpet of a warm turkey-red covered the newly varnished floor. Tulip-patterned wallpaper had faded from pink to a neutral beige, and they had let it alone. There was no radio here, no television. Those things were for the living room downstairs. But there were several easy chairs, a comfortable old sofa with slightly sagging springs, a large round table, moved down from leftover furniture in the attic, and two desks. Of course, there was also the family book collection filling the shelves; the encyclopedia, much-thumbed; and Dad's big unabridged dictionary. It was a room for reading and working—and dreaming.

Robin liked the old-fashioned mansard roof of the house, which gave added head space to this third floor, where servants had once had their rooms. Robin's own bedroom was, by choice, up here too. She especially liked the low windows cut into the roof—windows that grown-ups had to stoop to look through. Each had its own window seat, and Robin had curled up on one of these, where she could see outdoors and gather strength from the golden-green treetops warming in the afternoon sun of August.

To look at green, outdoor things usually made Robin feel more cheerful and hopeful, and she needed such encouragement now. From where she sat she could glimpse the queer old house next door and see that strange, unfriendly girl in the white dress down in the garden. What *was* she doing? But the strangeness of both house and girl would have to wait because there were more important matters going on within her own house, within this very room.

Mother sat in the wing chair she liked best, a torn shirt of Tommy's in her lap. Since Mother disliked mending, she always tried to combine it with something more interesting—like this conference. Her bronze-rimmed glasses matched the bronzy color of her hair, which was naturally curly, and worn short for comfort.

Her eyebrows were drawn down in a frown of concentration, her lips pursed doubtfully.

"At thirteen you ought to be able to make your own decisions and work at them, Robin," she said. "But I can't forget the piano lessons that were your last enthusiasm back in Maywood."

Tommy snickered and plucked at the red-gold forelock that no amount of combing seemed to remove from his eyes. All the Wards except Dad ran to reddish hair, Robin's being the reddest of the lot. Undoubtedly Tommy was enjoying the fact that for once he was not on the carpet, being judged.

In the depths of his green leather chair, Dad stretched his thin, long-legged person and sighed. For Robin this was the sound she minded most. The piano lessons, which she had desired so wholeheartedly for six months, had cost quite a lot of money, to say nothing of the purchase of a secondhand piano. The family had not brought the piano along from Maywood because Robin had long since lost interest in trying to play it.

She sought refreshment again from the warm green treetops and roused herself for both defense and attack.

Dad spoke before she was ready. "I'm afraid this has the earmarks of another whim, Robin. It has come on too suddenly. You haven't had time to make sure of what you want."

Robin turned her thoughts from the memory of the piano. "This is different! I'm sure. I was sure the minute we walked into Mr. Hornfeld's studio last evening and I saw the wonderful sculpture he has done. Besides, Mother knows this isn't sudden. I've always had fun working in clay."

Mother had reason to know this. She had taught art

classes in a grade school in Maywood and there was clay and plasticine to play with at home. Robin had modeled in clay for as long as she could remember, but it had never before struck her as being something important in her life.

There was now, however, more than before, the problem of money. In Chicago, Dad had been a biology teacher, and he had come here to be curator of biology at the local museum. It was work that appealed to him, since it would furnish an outlet for his own creative abilities. His teaching would consist mainly of lecturing to school classes that visited the museum, and he would also be able to follow his own research, create displays for the museum, and do a number of things he hadn't had a chance to do before. The move east had been expensive, and the Wards would have to spend cautiously for a time. Perhaps Mother would go back to teaching in the fall in order to help with the family income. At present money mustn't be spent foolishly.

Since their arrival, the Wards had met some of the museum staff, including Ira Hornfeld, who also lived in the small island community known as Catalpa Court. Mr. Hornfeld's work was famous and some of his sculptured pieces in terra-cotta, in marble and stone, or sometimes cast in bronze, were displayed by important museums around the country. Last evening he had invited the Wards to visit his studio and meet his wife and three children. The oldest boy, Julian, was a year older than Robin. Julian had been kind about showing her around and explaining some of the sculpture to her.

The feeling that had come over her as she looked at Mr. Hornfeld's work was something she had never experienced before. It was as if a shining, compelling urge had burst full-blown in her mind like a shower of fireworks sparks. Her fingers tingled with eagerness to make something beautiful that would match the dream in her mind. This surge of feeling was quite different from the urge she had felt to play the piano. When she had thought about music, she had imagined the neighborhood young people gathering around to listen to her and to sing the tunes she played so skillfully. Perhaps what she had wanted, if she were honest with herself, was to be admired and to show herself off. She had not yearned to produce musical sounds for their own sake.

This new feeling was not that sort of thing. This time she wasn't thinking about being a great sculptor like Mr. Hornfeld. The longing in her was much simpler. She wanted to put her hands into clay and create something beautiful and satisfying—something that grew out of her own feeling and talent. Perhaps this was the true test of whether she really wanted this. But she lacked the ability to put this feeling into words and explain it to her parents. She knew only that she must try—or remain unhappy forever. The feeling was as strong as that.

Last evening when Mother asked about the classes Mr. Hornfeld taught, Robin had listened intently. He told them that he had an adult class one evening a week at the museum and that, starting in September, he also held a small private class for young people in his own studio. This group was carefully chosen, and he took those few whom he believed had real talent. He was not interested in teaching arts and crafts, he said. He was concerned with the discovery and development of genuine talent. As she listened, Robin had begun to glow inwardly with excitement. She knew she had to be in that class.

To her respectful gaze, Mr. Hornfeld had seemed an

impressive figure—tall, with strong shoulders and arms from the work he did with heavy stone and marble. His thick, graying hair was combed back from a broad forehead and there was a slight, not unpleasant, curve to the bridge of his nose that was part of his racial heritage. His warm, brown eyes were surprisingly gentle, but Robin sensed that if he was angered, they would not remain so. The pointed gray beard added to his altogether distinguished appearance. When he spoke, though it was in a courteous, quiet manner, one nevertheless sensed his authority and assurance. He was not, Robin suspected, a man whom anyone would easily contradict or easily fool.

"I prefer to have no more than ten children in a class. Children from ten to fourteen years of age," he explained to Mother. "I expect each child who applies to work for some months ahead of time and bring in his best piece for me to judge. Then I choose the children who I feel have a true interest and the greatest creative possibilities."

Robin had hung on every word, though she said nothing at the time. The moment they left Mr. Hornfeld's to walk the few doors around the oval of Catalpa Court to their own house, she had announced her burning desire, her wish to be one of the chosen ten who would enter Mr. Hornfeld's class next month.

Her parents were considerably startled. At first they had attempted to discourage her from trying. It was too big a project, Mother said. She wasn't ready and couldn't be by next month—if ever. When Robin persisted and began to beg, Dad firmly cut her short and said the whole thing could wait overnight. They would think about it. Then they would hold a family conference and discuss it thoroughly the next day. Since

Map of Catalpa Court

Woods

Path

Woods

Path

Garage

Devery

Hedge

Empty House

Ward

Studio

Hornfeld

Wrecked House

Catalpa Trees

Simpson

Main Road

wheedling was forbidden in the Ward family, Robin knew she would have to wait. The final result was this meeting—which was not going at all well for her fervent hopes.

It was an undeniable fact that Robin had never proved herself able to stay with what she started. Her enthusiasm was a hot flame that usually lasted until such time as she discovered that her current ambition was going to take more effort than she expected. Thereupon she would give up. Tommy stuck to things better than Robin ever had, and Mother had just repeated this unhappy truth for the third time.

Robin swung around on the window seat and put her feet on the floor. "You don't understand! I stop doing something because I know that what I'm doing isn't any good. This would be different. This time I think I can make something good enough to show Mr. Hornfeld. Of course he might not take me. But couldn't I work at something anyway? Couldn't I try?"

There was a sudden warmth in Dad's bright blue eyes, a growing sympathy that gave Robin hope. Perhaps Mother was the most practical one, for all that Dad was a scientist. But it was Dad who felt things most deeply. Robin sensed that he might come to her aid.

"At least you have several weeks in which to attempt this," he said. "If your effort doesn't last that long, it won't matter. If it lasts and what you do isn't good enough, you will have to accept that. Do you think you can, Robin? How tough are you when it comes to serious disappointment? How good are you at bouncing?"

"I don't know," she told him honestly. "I guess I'll have to find out."

He smiled. "Yes, you'll have to find out. Part of succeeding at anything means standing up to the disappointments that are part of doing something well. The faster you learn, the better for you. Perhaps you should have the chance to prove that you can stick to something you really care about."

"Lumps of clay!" Tommy murmured, as though he could not understand this wish of his sister's. "Julian Hornfeld's going to be a newspaperman. I think that's what I'll be when I grow up—a reporter."

His words broke the tension and everyone laughed, knowing that Tommy Ward had found a new hero to follow.

"Good for you," Dad said. "I liked what I saw of Julian, though I think it's a bit early to settle on your life's work." He pushed himself regretfully from his chair. "Much as I like it here, I've got to get back to painting kitchen cupboards. This is Friday and I need to accomplish a good deal before my new job starts on Monday."

Robin flung herself across the room and into his arms, her long red braids flying. "Then I can try, Dad? At least I can try?"

He hugged her and looked at Mother. This time it was Mother who sighed because she still didn't believe in the project. But when she smiled at them both, Robin knew her mother would give every help possible from now on. Mother was like that. Once she made up her mind, she stuck to her chosen road without wavering. Robin wished a little of that quality would rub off on her.

The session had ended and Tommy jumped up and dashed for the door. "I'm going to tell Julian!" he shouted over his shoulder, and disappeared noisily down two flights of stairs before anyone could stop him.

Now there would be no chance to keep her plans

secret until she was sure they were going well, Robin thought, disgruntled. Dad winked at her encouragingly and Mother gave one of her brisk, everything-is-settled nods.

"It's probably just as well if Tommy does tell Julian," she said. "That way you'll be all the more committed to working at this. Let me know when you want some clay."

Robin nodded and said nothing. When her parents left and she had the big room to herself, she hugged herself ecstatically and danced across the turkey-red carpet. How wonderful the rest of this month was going to be! She loved Catalpa Court. Perhaps she would have Julian Hornfeld for a friend. Perhaps she would get to know his wonderful father a little better. And perhaps— oh, perhaps—she could create some lovely, exciting figure in clay so that she could be in Ira Hornfeld's class. With her whole being she longed for this, and she knew with a clarity she had never experienced before that this time she could not afford to fail. Before she took the crucial step of asking for that batch of clay, she must find a subject worthy of so important an effort. When she had found her subject, she must do justice to it. The future looked both alluring and frightening, but when she stopped to think of it, there wasn't much time.

From one of the windows at the side of the room a humming sound reached her from outdoors, distracting her from her thoughts. She knelt on a window seat so that she could look down into the front garden of the big house next door. She had already noted how different that house was from the others in the court. It had probably been built in the early 1900's, Mother had said, and it was not in the straight up-and-down style of the houses with mansard roofs. The builder of that house had fallen in love with balconies and turrets and ornate gingerbread decorations. The whole enormous structure was painted a sort of gingerbread color too—dreary and rather forbidding. It hunched itself in a grove of trees and was set farther back from the street than the Wards' yellow house.

On either side of the property was an enormously high, dark, untrimmed hedge. Of privet, Dad said. Across the front was a stone wall, with a wide gate through which carriages must once have been driven. On either side of the elaborate iron gate rose a stone post, on the top of which sat a stone lion. The two lions snarled at each other across the carriage drive, offering no welcome to anyone who might trespass through this unwelcoming entrance. At the rear stretched another stone wall, and beyond that lay an area of woods that ran behind the Ward property as well.

From the ground level it was impossible to see through the hedge, or over the high wall. But from this room, Robin had a perfectly clear view of the entire front lawn. She saw at once the source of the queer humming sound. It was that girl in the white dress again. Because she was moving, it was impossible to see her face clearly, but from other brief glimpses Robin judged her to be about her own age, or perhaps younger.

Her full dress fanned out about her as she whirled. She stood in the middle of the vast lawn, turning round and round with her arms out wide as if she were flying. As she turned she made a strange, tuneless sound that seemed to come out on a single high-pitched note. In a moment, Robin thought, she would get dizzy and tumble in a heap on the grass.

She did not, however, because something else happened first. Down the steps of the house came the tall, angry figure of a woman dressed in an old-fashioned brown tweed suit that seemed to match the house. She called out, "Stella, Stella!" as she ran across the lawn in the direction of the whirling girl. Though she was an elderly woman with hair that was nearly white, she moved spryly and reached the girl before she stopped turning. She grasped her by the arm, forcing her to an unsteady halt, and shook her crossly, scolding the while.

Robin could hear only the tone of the words, but her own sympathy went at once to the girl who was being treated so angrily. The woman thrust her in the direction of the front steps, never releasing her grasp. Now and then Stella stumbled and held back, but the woman in brown half pushed, half pulled her up the steps and into the house.

It was a disturbing scene to witness, and when it was over, Robin sat down on the window seat feeling upset and a little sick. She could not understand what had happened, but she had the feeling that in some queer way the girl in white was a prisoner in that ugly brown house; that she was held there in bondage by the stern brown woman with the white hair. The scene had all the earmarks of a fairy tale. A house with towers and an enchanted princess held under a spell. To say nothing of a wicked sorceress who would not let her go. Except that this was not a fairy tale. This was real.

Or was it?

The garden stood empty and all was quiet. The front door had been closed tightly. The many windows stared with blank eyes, revealing nothing. It was as though what Robin had seen could not possibly have happened.

(2)

A Slap for Julian

ROBIN CONTINUED to kneel on the window seat for a
while, looking down upon the garden next door, thinking over what had happened. The girl had not struggled
very hard in the woman's grasp. It was as though she
knew from the first touch on her arm that escape was
hopeless and she had given up. The whole thing was so
strange and puzzling that Robin decided to find out
about the people in the next house.

A scrabbling, snuffling sound outside the library door
made Robin smile. "Would you like to come in, Balmy
dear?" she called.

At once the snuffling turned to excited yelps, and
there was the eager thumping of a tail upon the floor.
Robin opened the door and Herr Binglebaum—Balmy,
for short—leaped upon her with all the fervor of a small,
loving dachshund. She caught him up and held him
close, short legs, floppy ears and all, not troubling to
dodge the kiss of a wet, pink tongue. Balmy was supposed to belong to the entire family, but they all knew
very well that he loved Robin best. After that, he loved
the whole world and everyone in it.

"Let's go out for a walk," she suggested. "You'd like
that, wouldn't you, Herr B.?"

21

Balmy squirmed from her arms in a flying leap and dashed for the stairs, showing proper enthusiasm at the word "out."

"Wait till I get your leash," Robin called.

Herr Binglebaum wanted to go out, and so did she. There was a great deal she needed to know about this neighborhood. Perhaps walking a friendly dachshund around the court might be a good way to start learning about one's neighbors.

Catalpa Court was part of an old Staten Island neighborhood and occupied the top of a steep ridge of hillside that ran up from the valley thoroughfare of Jersey Street. Another ridge of hills cut it off from New York harbor and the sight of Manhattan's towers. But parts of this hill looked toward New Jersey, and on clear days one could find unexpected views across Newark Airport clear to a row of distant Jersey hills.

Two or three blocks from the court ran a bus line that took the residents of the hill back and forth to ferries which ran every fifteen minutes between Staten Island and Manhattan. One of the things Robin liked most about living on Staten Island was the trip across the bay past the Statue of Liberty. It was strange to think that this old-fashioned area, with its fine tall trees and the imaginative architecture of another day, was part of New York City, being one of its five boroughs—the Borough of Richmond.

Catalpa Court was even more secluded than the rest of the hilltop, forming a sort of dead-end area of its own. From the main road a drive ran between square cement posts, one of which bore the name of the court. This drive branched right and left, and ran up each side of a long oval, to meet again at the rounded top. Down

the center of the oval were three smaller ovals, pleasantly grassy and planted with sturdy catalpa trees that
gave the court its name.

The top of the oval, farthest from the entrance, was
occupied by three houses. The house on the left, as one
faced the top of the oval from the court entrance, stood
empty and for rent. The center house was the Wards',
and the one in the right-hand corner, occupying the
largest area of ground, was the house in which the whirling girl lived. On the left-hand side of the oval, Julian
Hornfeld's house was first, and there were three others
running toward the entrance to the court. An equal
number of houses would have faced them on the other
side, but for one exception. It was this exception which
held Robin's attention as she left her own unfenced
lawn and walked past the high hedges and front wall of
the strange house next door. Balmy strained at his leash,
and she held onto him firmly.

The house that should have been next to the brown
house and that would have been directly across the oval
from Julian's was rapidly becoming not-a-house. That
is, the wreckers had come the day after the Wards' arrival and had been tearing it to bits and carting off the
broken timbers ever since. Robin had found herself
watching this destruction with a feeling of sadness. She
had not known the people who lived in it, yet she felt
unhappy about the demolishing of the house. Once it
had been a large, impressive home. Once it had been
loved and cared for. Families must have lived there in
happiness and in sorrow, setting their stamp upon every
room, upon the very grounds. Here before Robin's eyes
the great jaws of the wrecking machinery banged into
the wooden structure, taking great bites out of roofs and

gables. Bit by bit it had fallen into ruin with a great clatter and crashing, and with clouds of rising dust.

By this Friday afternoon the wreckers were nearly through. Only a solitary corner of the house remained, pitifully open for anyone to see. Robin stared up at sprigged yellow wallpaper in a second-floor room, and saw a bedraggled geranium in a pot on an inside windowsill. She held Balmy tightly and stood in the center of the oval directly across the drive from the wrecking machine. As she watched, the huge steel jaws bit a mouthful out of the tottering corner, and the tall crane swung away carrying debris to a truck. What remained trembled and wavered and then, as Robin held her breath, fell in upon itself with a resounding crash, dropping roof tiles, window glass, and splintered wood into a pile of kindling on the ground. One instant the red pot that held the geranium was there, and the next it was gone, shattered in the field of rubble below.

What remained looked like pictures Robin had seen of sites that had been bombed in the last war. An old tree lay uprooted, never to bloom again, and the smell of dust was thick and choking. Muddy ridges were left from yesterday's rain, being covered already by new dust and new rubble.

Because she did not like the look of this devastated place, she moved on around the oval to the house beyond the wrecked one. It belonged to the Simpsons, a family that had lived in the court for several generations. They had a daughter younger than Tommy, named Mary Lou, and an older boy called Brad. Brad was good at outdoor games and often gathered other boys from the neighborhood to practice with a bat and ball in the street in front of his house.

Tommy was over at the Simpsons' now, wearing a catcher's mitt almost as big as he was, while Brad good-naturedly pitched balls in his direction. Julian Hornfeld sat on the Simpson steps with Mary Lou beside him. Here, thought Robin, lay a promising source of information.

As she moved toward the Simpsons', Julian saw her and smiled. She returned his "hello" a little shyly. Unlike her brother, Robin was not especially good at rushing out to make friends. She felt friendly enough inside, and eager to know people, but it was hard to make this feeling come out toward others. Besides, she was afraid of being laughed at if she spoke up too quickly and expressed her somewhat individual thoughts. Quite often her notions did not seem to fit in with the ideas of other people. Then she was stared at, or even worse, snickered at. But Julian had been nice yesterday in his father's studio, and he didn't seem as rough and cheeky as Brad Simpson. She approached the steps where he sat, and smiled at him indirectly by smiling at Mary Lou.

Julian leaned over to make friends with the delighted Balmy and said nothing about what Tommy might have told him of Robin's project. She found that she could talk to the top of his head more comfortably than trying to talk when his dark, thoughtful eyes were upon her. Julian resembled his father quite a bit. He had the same general good looks and rather lean face. But he lacked his father's mature manner of authority, and although Robin was never quite sure what Julian was thinking, she found him less frightening than the well-known sculptor.

"Can you tell me who lives in the big brown house next door to ours?" she asked the top of Julian's dark head.

He answered easily, as if he were talking to Balmy, so that Robin wondered if he guessed how shy she felt with those whom she did not know very well.

"That's the Devery house," he said. "Mrs. Agnes Devery lives there. I believe her husband built it when they were married way back around 1910. Mrs. Simpson says he died in the First World War, and Mrs. Devery has lived there ever since."

Mary Lou was a squirming imp with two front teeth missing and a blond ponytail of which she was rather vain. She never stayed out of any conversation for long, Robin soon learned.

The little girl displayed the gap in her teeth and lisped through it with the assurance of a thoroughly spoiled child. "Mithuth Devery is a witch," she announced. "She puts spells on children and locks them up in her tower."

Julian let go of the dachshund and shook his head at Mary Lou. "That's silly. You mustn't go around saying things like that."

"Whoth going to stop me?" Mary Lou asked, never consistent in her lisping, so that Robin wondered if it was a pretense.

That was a good question and Julian looked help-lessly at Robin. Having eased into the conversation, she could accept his direct gaze with less shyness.

"I go over to cut grass for Mrs. Devery and do some weeding and odd jobs a couple of times a week," Julian explained. "She's an old lady in her seventies and not very happy, I think. Of course she's not a witch."

"I've seen a girl—" Robin began.

At once Mary Lou was back in the talk, her tongue going full tilt with a story about twelve-year-old Stella. Two days ago the girl had come to Mary Lou's eighth birthday party and she had been just awful. She had scowled and made faces, Mary Lou said, and she would not play any of the games with the other children.

Julian made a gesture intended to stem this outburst, but Mary Lou switched her ponytail at him and went right on.

"She even thlapped Julian right in hith fathe! And then she cried like a big baby and my mother had to take her home!"

Julian took hold of Mary Lou's ponytail gently but firmly. "Stop lisping," he said. "You don't have to. And stop talking like that about Stella."

A little bewildered, Robin looked from Mary Lou to Julian and saw to her distress that he had blushed a bright, fiery red at mention of the slap. She began to wish she had never spoken of Mrs. Devery or the girl who lived in the house next door.

Mary Lou continued, this time without any trace of a lisp. "You should see the pin Stella wore to my party! It was shaped like a star, and Mommy said it was made of real emeralds, with a diamond in the middle. Mommy said she couldn't imagine why a young girl was allowed to wear such a valuable pin to a children's party. But I guess Stella's not like other people. She's—"

This time Julian gave the ponytail a jerk, and Mary Lou choked off her words with a yelp.

"Stop it!" he told her firmly. "Don't say it! Don't say anything about her at all."

Mary Lou pulled her blond hair from his grasp and ran into the house calling out indignantly that Julian Hornfeld was a horrid boy and he was mean, mean, mean to girls.

Uncomfortable and embarrassed, Robin glanced at Julian and saw to her relief that his blush was fading. She would hate to have anyone see her blush like that and she wondered what lay behind the slap Stella had given him.

Julian managed a sheepish grin. "Don't pay any attention to Mary Lou. I'm only a little mean to girls."

"Mary Lou deserved it," Robin said earnestly.

"Thanks." His smile was friendly and lighted up his whole face. "About Stella—" he hesitated as if there was something he wanted to tell her. He shrugged. "Never mind. I don't want to talk about it. You'll find out if you get to know her."

"But who is she?" Robin asked. "Why is she living in that house with old Mrs. Devery?"

"Her mother is there too," Julian said. "They've been here about a month. They're Cuban refugees from Havana."

Before she could consider this surprising information and find further questions to ask, Julian ended the conversation by reaching out to catch a ball Tommy had missed. Then he got up from the steps and joined the game. He did not want to hear any more of her questions, Robin was sure, and now she wished she had not asked so many. She hoped she had not offended Julian Hornfeld so he wouldn't talk to her again.

"Come along," she said to Balmy, who was trying to get into the ball game.

Together they walked to the far end of the oval and stood looking out at cars going by on the main street.

They came back up the other side, passing Julian's house, where the younger Hornfeld children were playing in the front yard. They passed the house for rent next to the Wards', and were about to turn in at home when Robin happened to glance in the direction of the stone wall and the Devery lions. From here only the highest turrets of the house could be seen, but Robin discovered something that slowed her steps so that she could watch without seeming to.

Mrs. Devery, still in her severe brown suit that looked as though it would be warm on an August day, stood behind the open iron grillwork of the gate. She was staring through it in the direction of the open space where the wrecking crew loaded broken timbers into a truck, and smoothed out crushed rubble, their work nearly finished.

The thing that caught Robin's attention was not so much Mrs. Devery's interest in the lot where a beautiful old house had stood a week ago. It was the tight, angry expression on her face. Her mouth was drawn into so straight and thin a line that her lips were pinched white. Yet there was a flush of anger high on her prominent cheekbones. She had enormous eyes, set deep in their sockets beneath the bony, jutting brows above. From this distance Robin could not tell their color—the hollows shadowed them and made them dark. A breeze had begun to blow through Catalpa Court, stirring the dust of the wrecked house, stirring the white fluff of Mrs. Devery's hair. She wore it in an old-fashioned way that ended in a smooth, tight roll around the back of her head and was pinned down under a net that held all but a few front wisps flatly in place. As she reached up to smooth the front fluff that was stirring in the wind, she discovered Robin staring at her. She said nothing, but simply stared back haughtily with her searing gaze. Robin dropped her own eyes in embarrassment and hurried across the Ward front lawn, with Balmy dragging on his leash.

Goodness, what a look that had been! It had practically scorched, even at this distance. Robin felt increasingly sorry for the girl from Cuba who was staying in that house. A sudden understanding of the whirling and the humming dawned in Robin's mind. If Stella had escaped to the freedom of the open lawn, she might have whirled and hummed out of a sense of release from being shut in the house. Only to be stopped and led back to her prison again. Dragged back. Robin remembered that she had stumbled on the way.

What was it Mary Lou had started to say when Julian had stopped her? What had Julian been about to tell Robin himself? There was still some answer here that escaped her—something that was a possible key to the puzzle. Until she discovered what it was, she would continue to be baffled and curious.

(3)

Singing in the Night

THE PREVAILING WIND that blew out of the west across the North American continent and across New Jersey to Staten Island had strengthened in the twilight. The big screened-in front porch of the Wards' house was comfortable as the breeze dispelled the heat of the August day. The porch had been a later addition to the house and did not match the mansard type of architecture, but it was a wonderful spot for the family to gather in the cool of evening.

Dad was swinging idly in the hammock, tired after his painting and pounding. Mother was indoors mixing up a pitcher of her special pineapple-lemonade. Tommy had curled up in a porch chair, quiet for the moment because he was getting sleepy. Robin stood with her red head close to the screen, watching the constant thickening and thinning of firefly clusters in the garden. At her feet Balmy snored and whimpered to himself in a dream.

Strange how the fireflies would glow in a great mass over near the hedge that separated the Devery property from the Wards', then suddenly vanish and reappear in a thick cluster somewhere else. Sometimes there would be moments of darkness followed by scattered bits of light on the front lawn as the breeze fanned them out.

"Maybe I'll catch some fireflies and put them in a cage the way the Japanese do," Tommy said drowsily, but he made no move to leave his comfortable chair.

Dad had begun to snore lightly, almost in rhythm with Herr Binglebaum. Robin said nothing. A most curious firefly had just caught her attention.

At first she thought it was a rather large one, down toward the Catalpa Court oval. Then she realized that it was not a firefly, but a light moving about the empty rubble of the wrecked house. Someone was over there. This deserved investigation.

"I'll take Balmy for a walk," she announced idly. "All right, Dad?"

Dad came out of his dozing, considered the matter, and nodded. That was one good thing about the court. It was like a small private world that could shut out possible nighttime dangers from the outside world. There was no through traffic here, and the cars that belonged to the various houses came and went slowly because the dead-end road around the oval was used as much for a playground as for a drive. A stranger moving about Catalpa Court would be immediately conspicuous and likely to be questioned. The oval itself was well lighted, with children playing all over it until bedtime. Robin could hear Brad Simpson shouting to someone out there, and a dog was barking.

She clipped Balmy's leash to his collar and walked across the grass so they would make as little noise as possible. No lights were visible in the upper towers of the Devery house, though a light set in an old carriage lamp standard burned beside the iron gateway. Robin went past the snarling lions quickly, as though she might attract their attention if she lingered. Ahead, the flashlight still searched among the shards of broken pottery and glass and flowerpots that the wreckers had left behind.

"Be quiet, Balmy," Robin whispered, and for once the dachshund heeded her command and did not make a sound as they moved in the direction of the vacant lot.

Robin did not want to be seen by the person with the flashlight, so she sought for a roundabout approach. In the light cast by a streetlamp she found a rough path that led between the far Devery hedge and the area of the wrecked house. The path dropped downhill, edging a large rear garden, then wound away into the woods that ran behind Devery property. There were trees all along the path and it was darker here.

Slowly Robin and Balmy circled behind the moving torch in order to approach from the shadowy garden, where she could view what was happening unseen. She had a strong feeling that the person with the light had something to do with the puzzle of the Devery house.

As the path turned toward the woods, she left it and moved among weeds and uncut grass where the wreckers had not turned up the earth. A small structure stood alone in the middle of the long slope and Robin saw that it was a small summerhouse. Its octagonal sides were sheltered by the overhang of the roof that pointed upward into the growing dusk. Doorway and open windows were overgrown with vines and lost in shadow. It would be a perfect place to hide in and watch as the flashlight moved about the front of the empty lot.

Stepping carefully over uneven ground, Robin moved toward the summerhouse. Balmy snuffled along beside her as quietly as she could reasonably expect, and she forgot to hold his leash tightly. Without warning he pulled it from her hand and dashed in the direction of the little house, barking with eagerness and joy. Robin tried to whistle him back, but he was making too much noise to hear her. All chance of secrecy was gone for good.

Balmy reached the door and hurled himself into the dark interior with yelps of enthusiasm. There was an exclamation of dismay from within, and a figure appeared in the doorway with Balmy yapping welcome at

his heels. Robin could only stand where she was and stare in consternation. The man who thrust Balmy aside with an unfriendly foot and dashed down the steps was short and rather fat. He had a round white moon face and a bald head. He did not pause to look around, but ran clumsily toward the dark row of trees that sheltered the path Robin had found. There he disappeared into the shadows, and Robin could not tell whether he had followed the path through the woods or was standing still, hidden in the shadows, watching.

Balmy began to whine. He had caught his leash in the crack of a splintered step, and Robin bent to release him, scolding softly the while. When his leash was firmly in her grasp again, she led him up three steps into the small structure that the wreckers had not troubled to demolish. There was nothing inside except a rough wooden floor and benches that ran beneath latticework windows. As she had thought, it would have been a good place from which to look out without being seen. Indeed, that was what the fat little man with the moon face must have been doing. Robin had not liked the way he had run off, nor the way in which he had kicked at Balmy. She stood on a wooden seat and thrust away a curtain of vines so that she could look up the hill, expecting the flashlight to be gone after all the noise.

To her surprise the circle of light still moved about the rubble. The illumination of a streetlamp permitted her to make out the figure who held the torch. It was Mrs. Devery. Inch by inch the woman seemed to be moving around over the crushed surface the wreckers had combed over the lot before they took away their steel jaws for good. In one hand she carried her flashlight, while in the other she held a cane. With this she

poked about through wood splinters and broken glass
and shattered pottery. If she had heard Balmy's barking
and the sound of the fat man running away, she had
apparently paid no attention.

What in the world could she be looking for? Robin
wondered. What could she hope to find in that mass of
pulverized wreckage?

But as Robin pondered this, the old lady suddenly
bent toward the ground and picked something up. The
light was too dim for Robin to tell what it was, but she
saw Mrs. Devery switch off her torch and move, erectly
purposeful now, in the direction of her house.

"You be quiet!" Robin whispered fiercely to Balmy.
The little dog's friendliness made him hard to control.
He had only meant to greet the fat man lovingly, having
no sense of discrimination. He might leap with equal
enthusiasm upon Mrs. Devery, who, Robin suspected,
would not welcome his advances.

Robin had just started after her when a movement near the thick darkness of trees and path caught her eye. The white flash of a moon face was revealed briefly by the streetlamp. Then nothing was there. But she knew that the fat man had stayed to watch Mrs. Devery. Now, however, he had disappeared, and Robin, listening intently, heard a faint rustle of bushes where the path wound around through woods behind the Devery house.

Catalpa Court stood empty and quiet. Most of the children had gone inside to bed, and when Mother's voice called suddenly across the empty oval, the sound was startling.

"Robin? Where are you? Come home for lemonade."

"Coming," Robin answered, thinking ruefully that there was not much possibility of doing anything secret around here tonight.

She followed the curving sidewalk past the Devery front gate and saw that it was fastened with a large padlock. The iron grillwork that was all decorative scrolls and curls in its lower part rose into pointed, forbidding spears at the top. In the lamplight the hollow eyes of the lions seemed to turn in Robin's direction, and she suddenly took to her heels and ran for the safety of home, with Balmy puffing along in great glee behind her on his short legs.

The pineapple-lemonade tasted wonderfully cool and refreshing. Robin sipped gratefully and said nothing about her adventure. There was nothing to say. Nothing of the key to what was going on had been given her. The whole episode was still a big blank question mark and made no sense.

Later, when she went upstairs to her own room to get ready for bed, she put the whole affair determinedly from her mind. There were more important things to think about, though she had allowed herself to be distracted from them for a good part of the evening.

Perhaps she had postponed her thinking because the subject made her a little fearful. The first step in her plan was to decide what it was she would model in clay to submit to Mr. Hornfeld in an effort to get into his class. This was something she had to think about soon, whether it frightened her or not.

She looked a bit vaguely about the third-floor bedroom she had chosen for herself. Whereas the library at the front corner of the third floor occupied a large space, this room was much smaller and took up only a portion of this rear corner. Mother thought it had probably been a maid's room and suggested that Robin might enjoy something larger. But Robin liked the coziness of walls tight around her, and she liked the wallpaper with its yellow jonquil design. True, the wallpaper wasn't in good condition, but it had a feeling of being part of the life that had once existed in this house a long time ago.

Most of all, Robin liked the French doors that opened upon her own private balcony at the back of the house. Here she could be up among the treetops, where robins nested and squirrels ran from limb to high limb. In the daytime she could look down through the branches to their own backyard where Balmy had his kennel and where Tommy was building some weird contraption out of wood and metal and plastic that he said was a submarine.

The balcony drew her now, and she went outside in the soft darkness. The floor felt rough and splintery under her bare feet, but she didn't mind. In her pajamas she leaned upon the wooden rail, and her red braids hung over her shoulders. It was a good firm rail—Dad had tested it when they first moved in.

What could she choose for her project? she wondered wistfully. Where might she find her inspiration? From the backyard came the sound of Herr Binglebaum talking to himself with his own small yelps and whimpers, and she wondered if a dachshund would make a worthy subject. She certainly loved Balmy enough. She could make a darling clay dachshund, she felt sure. But even as she considered this, she rejected the idea. She did not want her subject to be funny. Much as she loved Balmy, she could not do a modeling of him without the humor that was sure to creep in. His very dignity was funny in so oddly shaped a dog. Her choice must be something important, something serious. Balmy wouldn't do.

A sound of singing came to her through the treetops, and for a moment she thought someone in another house had turned on a radio. Then she realized that there was no underlying accompaniment of music, but only a voice singing in Spanish. She recognized a tune she had heard many times on the radio—"Estrellita."

It sounded utterly melancholy now, as if there were tears ready to brim over in the singer's voice. She was surprised to find that the sound came from the direction of the Devery house. This rear balcony projected toward a front corner of the other house, so that the two were fairly close. In the daytime she had been able to see the Devery house clearly from this high balcony. Now she could see nothing because no upstairs lights showed through the trees, though lamps were lit in one of the big downstairs rooms, gleaming faintly behind closed draperies.

The voice drifted to her from one of the dark upper

rooms—a young voice, and very sad. Listening to it made a lump rise in Robin's throat. She knew it must be the voice of the girl in the white dress—the girl named Stella, who had once lived in Cuba. "Stella" meant star, and "Estrellita" meant "little star." This girl had worn an emerald and diamond star on her dress when she had gone to Mary Lou's party, the party at which she had slapped Julian Hornfeld, who did not seem like the sort of boy one would ever want to slap.

The strangeness overwhelmed Robin as she stood listening. In another moment she felt she would be crying too. Yet she did not know why she wanted to cry, except that there was some quality in the lovely voice that broke her heart as she listened to it, a quality that ached with pain and sorrow and terrible loss.

Before her tears spilled, however, the upper room in the other house sprang suddenly into light as if a curtain had gone up in a theater. The voice broke off with a faint sob, and Robin could see quite clearly what was happening in the other room. The blinds were not drawn and a single, cheaply shaded bulb hung down from the center of the ceiling. Near the door stood a woman with her hand on the light switch she had just touched. The scene seemed amazingly close, as if it were magnified, with all else around it dark. Robin could see how pretty the woman was—a dark, Spanish prettiness. This, of course, must be Stella's mother. The girl wore a long white nightgown, and she had evidently been sitting up in bed singing her heart out there in the unlit room.

The woman said something softly, and Robin caught the cadence of Spanish words as she came toward the girl on the bed, her arms held out in tender pleading.

But the girl turned her face away and drew back when her mother's arms touched her.

There was something heartbreaking and terrible about the scene. Robin realized in a flash that she was watching something she had no business watching. There was trouble and unhappiness in the Devery house. Trouble and unhappiness lay in that room between mother and daughter, and no stranger had any right to watch.

Moving softly, as though they might hear her, Robin slipped through the glass doors and back into her room. There she turned out the light and got into bed. A pattern of brightness rippled across her ceiling as the light bulb in Stella's room swayed in a breeze. Through Robin's mind the tune of the song wailed endlessly, and when she finally fell asleep tears were wet upon her pillow.

(4)

The Emerald Star

EMOTIONS OFTEN CHANGE by morning. A sorrow that seems unbearable in the darkness often disappears with the coming of the sun. Robin awakened the next morning with no thought in her mind except that she was terribly hungry and that the fragrance of bacon drifting up to her from the kitchen was not to be resisted.

Until the pangs of emptiness subsided, she thought of very little except eating. She did not talk much at breakfast, even when she was no longer hungry, because as soon as her appetite was satisfied, a plan began to form in her mind. Yesterday had been one of the strangest days she had ever lived. She suspected that if she tried to tell about it, Mother would make the whole thing seem simple and down-to-earth. Robin didn't want that to happen. In spite of the strange, almost frightening aspects of her adventure—such as Balmy's encounter with that fat man last night—Robin did not want the feeling of mystery to be dispelled. She wanted to work this out for herself. The only person she could imagine consulting was Julian Hornfeld. But she felt she did not know him well enough and she couldn't bear to have him laugh at her.

The day was going to be hot, and she changed into

cool, blue denim shorts and a sleeveless white blouse. Then she went downstairs and out of the back door to the fenced-in yard. Balmy begged to go with her, but she decided it was wiser to leave him at home for this particular venture.

She left the yard and walked along the automobile drive beside the tall Devery hedges. In one place on her way to the front of the house, she found that there was a thin spot low down in the hedge. She dropped to her knees and peered with interest into the next-door garden. The girl in white was nowhere in sight, nor was Mrs. Devery or the pretty woman who must be the girl's mother. Only Julian Hornfeld was in view, busily running a lawn mower back and forth across the enormous expanse of grass. He wouldn't hear her if she called to him, and he did not see her observing him through the hedge.

She got up and walked to the front sidewalk. Only then did she see Stella at the Devery front gate. The girl's fingers grasped the grillwork as she stared out through a curving iron design. This morning she wasn't dressed in white, but wore blue jeans and a red shirt. Her hair was not black like her mother's, but dark brown with bright highlights in it, and she wore it short and smooth, like a small cap about her head. It seemed straight and fine, and there was a fringe of bangs across her forehead. She was a rather pretty girl, but there was some strangeness about her, perhaps a singularity in the solemn way in which she stared through the bars of the gate. She seemed to be looking directly at Robin, and on impulse Robin smiled at her and waved. The girl did not smile or wave in return. She continued to stare sullenly and without any response.

Chilled by such unfriendliness, Robin turned her back and went out into the bright morning sunlight of Catalpa Court. The chocolate-colored trunks of stubby catalpa trees down the center oval rose into thickly spreading, heart-shaped leaves that offered shade, but she chose the glaring sun of the open area the wreckers had left. Never mind if that strange girl watched her every move. If Stella did not choose to be friendly, Robin would pay no attention. She had a plan to carry out.

Hardly anyone was about as yet this Saturday morning. She could hear children's voices from inside the nearest house, and a man down the block was washing his car in a driveway. It was nice to have the place almost to herself.

Sun shone through a broken place in the roof of the summerhouse down the hill, but the octagonal building seemed empty of any watcher this morning. Robin went to the section of the lot where Mrs. Devery had been digging and began to stir the rubble about with one toe of her sneakers. The result was only to soil her shoe. She turned up nothing except bits of broken wood and glass and brick. She wasn't sure exactly what else she hoped to find. If there had been anything to be found, Mrs. Devery had probably found it last night. But Robin meant to try anyway.

What she needed was a stick to dig with. She turned to the prone tree the wreckers had destroyed, and broke off a short branch, feeling as though she ought to apologize to the poor thing for what had been done to it.

This improvised digger helped a little, and she was able to make furrows in the pulverizèd mass. But she found nothing of interest. When at length she glanced carelessly toward the Devery place, she saw the girl still there at the gate, apparently watching her every move. Robin wondered if perhaps she did not speak English. That might make her seem shy and unfriendly. Robin herself knew what it was like to be shy with strangers. Mother had said more than once that there were times when her holding back made her seem unwilling to make friends when that wasn't what she intended. Perhaps if she found anything of interest in this broken stuff, she would take it over to show Stella. That might help them both to be less shy. She could not forget the haunting sadness of the voice she had heard singing last night. She could not shake off the feeling that no matter how this girl behaved, here was someone who was lonely, perhaps in trouble and in need of a friend.

Robin went to work at her digging with a new will, and suddenly her stick struck something embedded in the crushed rubble. She poked it loose and bent to pick up an object made of some greenish, discolored metal, small and rather heavy. The underside was a circle, encrusted with earth. When she tapped the object against a brick, the embedded dirt fell out, leaving a hollow in the metal. The other side was knobby, and when she tapped and poked at it a bit, the knob took on a shape like that of some sort of animal.

As she worked, a feeling that someone was watching her intently came over Robin. She whirled around and stared at the summerhouse, but it was still empty. Next she studied the far row of trees that had been lost in shadow last night. Had she again caught the movement of something over there? The flicker of someone quickly stepping behind a tree? Or was she imagining things? She remembered the fat man who had run away last night and hoped that she would never see him again. Stella still watched from behind her gate—perhaps that was all she had sensed.

"Hey, Robin, what have you found?" Tommy's voice shouted, startling her.

Robin sighed as her brother came toward her from the oval. A fine chance she had of keeping any sort of secret with Tommy around to publish it. Perhaps he was the one she had felt watching her. She held the object out to him in exasperation.

"All right—you tell me what it is."

Tommy could be surprisingly knowledgeable at times. He pursed his mouth and wrinkled his snubbed nose. "It looks like a lid to something," he said, turning it around in his fingers. "Brass, I think. You can tell if you clean it up. Maybe it's Chinese or something. That could be a temple dog sitting on the top. Or an Oriental lion with a ball between its paws."

Robin took her treasure back in some astonishment.

"Thank you, Sherlock Holmes," she said, and Tommy grinned.

"Maybe I'll do some treasure-hunting myself," he said and picked up the stick she had discarded.

Robin returned to the sidewalk, the small brass object in her hand, and started deliberately toward the Devery gate. But before she reached it, the girl seemed to sense her intent and she left her post to disappear inside the grounds. So that was that—she was definitely unfriendly. Feeling disappointed and a little annoyed, Robin returned to her own front lawn, wondering what to do next. From the backyard came the sound of Balmy whining, unhappy at being left alone and announcing the fact to the world. Robin paused beside the stone birdbath in the middle of the lawn and set the brass object on a ledge underneath, where she could retrieve it later. Then she went toward the gate to the backyard to let Balmy out.

He was waiting for her, his forepaws on the wire netting of the fence, his straight tail wagging madly. She opened the gate without expecting what happened next. Yelping with delight, Balmy did a corkscrew twist in midair and dived for the open air of freedom, streaking through the gate and down the drive. Robin ran after him, calling his name. There were laws on Staten Island about unleashed dogs and she did not want him to get into trouble. Balmy cared nothing about laws and he loved a good chase. Halfway down the drive he found the low opening in the Devery hedge, and in an instant he had wriggled through into the next-door garden.

In dismay Robin dropped to her hands and knees and looked through the hole. Julian was far across on the other side, his back turned, his mower making an uproar. Stella stood beside a path that led across the lawn and Balmy was leaping joyfully round and round her, with an occasional friendly nip at her blue-jeaned legs. That Stella stood frozen in terror was evident by the look on her face.

"The dog won't hurt you!" Robin called, but her words were drowned out by the sound of the lawn mower.

The girl dropped suddenly to the grass, drawing her knees up to her forehead and hiding her face against them. She wound her arms about herself as if in protection, like a tortoise trying to retreat into a shell. Balmy liked this. He leaped up to kiss her bare arm with a wet tongue, whimpering with pleasure over finding a new friend at such an available level. The lawn mower stopped whirring, and Julian turned and saw what was happening. Robin called out again that Balmy wouldn't hurt anyone. She squeezed through the hedge and ran across the grass toward the hunched-up girl.

But before either she or Julian reached Stella, Balmy settled the whole affair himself. He stopped yelping and flying dizzily in a circle. Instead he stood still and nuzzled his wet nose winningly into Stella's hand. She raised her head and the terror went out of her face. Hesitantly she reached toward Balmy and touched his small, friendly body. She found his ears and began to scratch behind them lightly, then stroked his satiny brown hide right down to his tail, while Balmy wriggled in delight over such attention.

"What's his name?" Stella said, using perfectly good English in which there was no trace of an accent.

"His full name is Herr Binglebaum, but we call him Balmy," Robin said, watching uneasily. She had never seen anyone behave in such a terrified manner over a small, friendly dog. There had been something so extreme about the girl's fear that it had been alarming to see.

Julian left his grass-cutting and came over to watch. "He's a dachshund," he told Stella.

The explanation seemed to imply that Stella was either very young or rather stupid, and Robin glanced at him in surprise. Surely there were dachshunds in Cuba, or she would have seen pictures of them so she could recognize one when she saw it.

Stella raised her head and smiled at Julian, and the look made Robin catch her breath. The sullen, unfriendly expression had vanished, and so had the terror. When she smiled, this girl was radiantly beautiful. She had a rounded chin with a cleft in it, and a wide, sensitive mouth that lifted in a marvelous smile. Her hazel eyes were lovely, with dark lashes fringing them. Lovely and a little strange, though Robin was not sure why. One thing was certain. If Stella had slapped Julian at Mary Lou's birthday party, she had since forgiven him for whatever had made her angry.

Robin spoke to the girl on impulse. "I heard you singing last night," she said. "Such a beautiful, sad song."

Stella turned her head in Robin's direction. "You must live next door?"

What a strange question to ask. Surely Stella would know they had moved in a week ago. She had certainly been watching Robin this morning and must have seen her come from next door.

A voice called suddenly from the broad veranda of the Devery house, and Robin turned to see Mrs. Devery standing there.

"Boy!" she called, addressing Julian. "Why aren't you cutting the grass?"

"I'm almost through, Mrs. Devery," Julian said politely, and returned to his lawn mower.

In an instant the look of happiness disappeared from Stella's face. Her hand had darted to her blouse. She fumbled at something and brought it away in her hand.

"Please," she said to Robin. "Please hold this for me. Just until she's gone."

The extended hand did not quite reach her own and

Robin had to bend to take the object from Stella's fingers. Again the hazel eyes looked at her with a certain strangeness. The truth came to Robin in an instant. The truth that Mary Lou had started to speak yesterday, the truth that Julian had stopped her from putting into words and held back himself. This girl with the haunting smile and the lovely hazel eyes was blind. There could be no other explanation. Robin reached for Stella's hand. Her fingers closed about a small object and felt the prick of a pin.

Mrs. Devery came briskly down the steps toward them, glancing at Julian to make sure he was working, then proceeded straight toward the place where Stella sat on the grass fondling Balmy. The word "witch" popped into Robin's mind, and she had a momentary desire to run. She thrust back the foolish impulse and stood her ground. After all, she was not as young as Mary Lou.

Mrs. Devery bore down upon them, her smooth, white hair shining in the sun. She wore her most autocratic manner.

"Who are you?" she demanded of Robin the moment she was near enough to speak. "Where did that dog come from?"

Robin closed her fingers about the pin Stella had given her and felt the points of a star in her hand. "I'm Robin Ward," she said. "We've just moved in next door."

"And this is Herr Binglebaum, Robin's dog," said Stella, holding the willing Balmy tightly in her arms.

"How did you get in here?" Mrs. Devery demanded of Robin.

"Through the hedge." Robin waved her hand.

"Balmy got away from me and I had to come through after him. I'm sorry. He didn't mean to frighten Stella."

Mrs. Devery had a thin, high-bridged nose. The nostrils had a pinched look as if she spent a great deal of time sniffing at people in a superior fashion. She sniffed at Robin now.

"Please take your dog and go home. But not through the hedge. The hole will have to be mended. Go out through the gate, if you please. I do not welcome uninvited visitors in my grounds."

Robin managed to extricate Balmy from Stella's grasp, careful not to let go of the pin or reveal it in her hand. Across the lawn the mower had stopped humming. Julian was leaning upon its handle, watching and listening.

Mrs. Devery noted the silence. "Boy!" she said without glancing in his direction. At once the mower started up again. This time Mrs. Devery's sniff was louder and more disdainful. "Jews!" she said. "We never had Jews in Catalpa Court in the old days."

Robin gasped softly, holding Balmy's squirming body close in her arms. She felt shocked to her very fingertips. In the Ward family no one would ever think of speaking of Jewish people in such a fashion. The Wards had lots of Jewish friends. But it was Stella, surprisingly, who stepped up to the battle line. She rose from her place on the grass, steadied herself, feet apart, and spoke in a light, quick voice that had a hint of anger in it.

"I don't suppose you had Cubans here in the old days either!" she cried.

A flush spread across Mrs. Devery's finely wrinkled cheeks. "Don't talk like that! You're not a Cuban. Your father was my son and that makes you an American."

"I was born in Cuba," Stella went on, her anger growing. "My mother is a Cuban and my other grandmother, my *abuela,* who lived in Havana, was a Cuban. I hate it here. I don't want to be an American!"

She looked as if she might burst into tears, but she managed not to. She turned with trembling dignity in the direction of the house and went toward it as if she could see perfectly well.

"Wait!" Mrs. Devery commanded. "You mustn't go stumbling around by yourself. You'll get hurt."

She started after Stella, but the girl moved more quickly than she did. To Robin's astonishment, she walked with the certainty of a sighted person toward the house and went up the steps and inside before her grandmother could reach her. Was she mistaken, after all? Robin wondered. Could the girl really see?

Mrs. Devery had forgotten everyone but her granddaughter, and as Robin stood staring after her, she too disappeared through the big front door and there was a rattle of glass as it closed after her.

Julian, having finished his last strip of grass, had put the mower away. He came toward Robin, smiling ruefully. At least, she thought, the sound of the mower had hidden the word Mrs. Devery had spoken with such ugly contempt.

"So now you know about Stella," Julian said.

Robin nodded. "She's blind, isn't she? Why didn't you tell me?"

"Because she's a person," said Julian strangely. "It didn't seem fair to give her a label before you'd met her."

"Isn't everyone a person?" Robin puzzled over his words. "I don't know what you mean."

"Of course everyone's a person. But sometimes we

act as if people were only labels. Like deaf, or blind, or lame. We forget about the person and only see the word."

Robin smiled at him warmly, beginning to understand. Julian Hornfeld was not like anyone she had ever known and she liked him a great deal. With sudden perception it came to her that there were other kinds of labels too—like the one the old woman had used about Julian. Mrs. Devery had put a label between herself and the whole fascinating Hornfeld family. She had cheated herself of knowing them because of a word she did not like. The word "Jews."

The star pin was pricking Robin's fingers and she held it out to this tall, slender boy with the dark eyes which seemed to see so much. On her palm the green stones that ran to the tip of each star point shone brightly in the sunlight. A big clear stone in the center flashed dazzling rainbow lights.

"What shall I do with this?" she asked.

"The stones do look real, don't they?" Julian said. "Not that I've seen many emeralds or diamonds that big. You'd better take it home and put it in a safe place until you can return it to Stella. Don't get her into any more trouble now."

Robin curled her fingers uneasily about the pin. Did it belong to Mrs. Devery, and had Stella been wearing it against her wishes? If these were real emeralds and a big diamond, the pin was undoubtedly valuable and she didn't like having it in her possession. What if she lost it, or something happened to it? She held the struggling Balmy under one arm, and the pin tightly in the fingers of her right hand as she and Julian moved toward the front gate.

Something else puzzled her, and she put the thought into words. "I don't understand how Stella could walk straight to the house and find her way up the steps without fumbling, just as if she could see."

Without turning toward the house, Julian paused on the way to the gate. "Listen!" he said.

Robin stopped beside him. The feathery leaves of a mimosa tree whispered nearby, lifting plumy pink blossoms in the wind that always seemed to blow on Staten Island. Then she heard something else—a light, tinkling, musical sound she had not noticed before. She turned and looked toward the veranda. There, hanging from the ceiling above the front steps, were wind-bells made of bits of glass that stirred and tinkled when the slightest breath of air touched them.

"Of course!" Robin cried in delight. "She would hear that sound, wouldn't she, and know exactly where to go? Were the bells always there? I mean before she came?"

Julian shook his head. "Mother had them at home. She sent them over for me to put up above the front steps so that Stella could find her way whenever she was in the garden."

"That's wonderful!" Robin said. "How did your mother happen to think of that?"

They continued toward the gate as Julian answered. "Dad has taken several blind people in his sculpturing classes—both grown-ups and children. Mother was especially interested in his work with them. It's too bad Mrs. Devery doesn't believe in the bells."

"What do you mean—she doesn't believe in them?"

"She didn't want me to put them up. She has that label 'blind' written so big in her mind that she thinks Stella can't do anything by herself. That's part of the trouble."

"I knew there was trouble," Robin said. "I could feel it in everything I saw and heard about that house."

They had reached the iron gate, and as Julian pulled it open Robin stepped between the two lions on their high stone posts. At that instant someone spoke to her from outside the gate. She jumped in fright, as though one of the lions had addressed her, and struck her right hand against an iron crossbar. The star pin went flying from her grasp and fell into the grass near the sidewalk. As Robin stared after it in dismay, she saw that the person who had startled her was the same fat, bald man who had run out of the summerhouse last night.

Robin set Balmy down and knelt to search for the pin. Her heart was pounding in her chest, both at the thought of losing it, and because she had been so startled. Julian closed the gate and came to help, but it was the man who found the pin. He fished it out of the grass and stood looking at it, shaking his head.

"My, my, what a pretty bauble!" he said. "You must have bought out the dime store!"

(5)

The Shining Dream

ROBIN SNATCHED the star pin back from him without troubling to explain. She knew with all her heart that she didn't like this man. In the sunlight his bald head and round face looked pink and moist with perspiration. One cheek was plumped out as he sucked noisily on something in his mouth. In one hand he held a candy packet which he thrust toward Robin.

"Lemon drops," he said. "Have one."

Although she disliked him, Robin did not know how to refuse gracefully. When she had thrust the pin deeply into a pocket in her shorts, she took a sticky lemon drop and put it reluctantly into her mouth. Julian had better sense. He shook his head when the candy was offered him. Balmy, having scampered a short distance off, bounced back with his tail wagging and offered his friendship without hesitation to the man with the lemon drops. Robin wished for his leash and tried without success to pull the dachshund away.

Clearly the fat man did not care much for dogs. He held Balmy off with one foot and nodded toward the Devery house.

"I saw what happened in there just now," he said. "That poor little blind girl! What a terrible tragedy!"

Robin was pleased to see that Julian regarded this

58

stranger with no more liking than she felt for him. He stared at him quite pointedly.

"Have you moved into Catalpa Court, Mr. er—uh—?" he asked.

For a moment the man seemed taken aback by this direct question. He stared at the packet in his hand and grinned slyly.

"You can call me Mr. Lemon," he said, and did not answer the question about moving in.

"There aren't any rooming houses in the court," Julian told him.

The fat man looked as though his feelings were hurt. He thrust the eager Balmy away for a last time, nodded at them abruptly, and took himself and his lemon drops off in the direction of the path through the woods that he had used last night. Robin watched him go, feeling increasingly troubled.

"I don't like that man," she said, spitting out the lemon drop. "But how do I know I'm not giving him one of those labels you mentioned? Maybe what I don't like is the word 'stranger.'"

Julian laughed out loud and the ringing sound was pleasant to hear. It wasn't the sort of laughter that poked fun. It laughed with Robin, not at her.

"Good for you!" he said. "You learn faster than I do. But I don't think we have to like everybody. It depends on the person. If I picked out a word like 'stranger' and disliked everyone who was new to the court—like you, for instance—I'd be on the wrong track too. This Mr. Lemon—though I don't think that's his real name—is as much of a person as any of us. But for me he's a person I don't like. Even if he was introduced as an old friend of my father's, I still wouldn't like him."

Robin agreed, feeling reassured. As Julian started in

the direction of his own house, she walked with him toward the Wards', carrying Balmy once more. She was thinking again of the girl next door.

"It must be an awful thing to be blind," she mused. "I feel terribly sorry for Stella Devery."

The sharpness of Julian's tone surprised her. "You haven't any right to feel sorry for her. If you're sorry for her, that means you're putting yourself above her. Anything can be terrible if we make it terrible, or if we let other people keep telling us how terrible it is. I hope Stella has more sense than to be sorry for herself."

Robin hurried to her own self-defense. She did not like to be put down in the way Julian had just put her down. Besides, she felt a little hurt that this boy who had seemed kind and friendly should suddenly talk to her in such a way.

"How can you think Stella has much sense when she slapped you at Mary Lou's party?" she asked bluntly.

This time Julian did not blush, though Robin watched for any telltale sign of pinkness in his face. Instead, he grinned at her wryly.

"Maybe that was my own fault. Sometimes I get mad and snap at people. The way I did just now with you."

This was as near as he meant to come to an apology, she knew. He gave her a casual, "So long," and went quickly away as though he did not want to talk to her any more. She watched him go, feeling startled and confused.

What had he meant about blindness not being terrible? That made no sense at all. It would be unkind not to feel sorry for Stella Devery. Her pity wasn't due to any feeling of superiority toward Stella, she felt sure. Nevertheless, Julian had given her something more to puzzle over. Perhaps that was why he seemed interesting. He kept stirring up her mind, making her think about things she had never considered before. You couldn't take anything for granted around Julian Hornfeld.

Balmy wriggled rebelliously under her arm, and Robin gave him a firm squeeze. "Stop it! You are a very bad dog, but I love you. If you hadn't misbehaved, perhaps I wouldn't have had a chance to meet Stella Devery. Just the same, you're going right into your own backyard and you're going to stay there."

On the way across the lawn she remembered the brass lid she had found, and stopped to reach beneath the birdbath to the stone ledge where she had put it. There was nothing there. That seemed puzzling, but there was probably some simple explanation. She carried Balmy into the backyard, closed the gate, and set him down. Tommy was hard at work on his submarine.

"Did you take away that brass thing I found this morning?" she asked. "I put it under the birdbath."

Tommy barely looked at her. "Of course not. What would I want it for?"

"Maybe to use on your submarine," Robin said.

He wrinkled his nose in disgust. "Don't be silly! Besides, this isn't a sub, it's a helicopter."

Robin gave up and went into the house through the back door. The disappearance wasn't important. Perhaps some child had taken it. Or perhaps she had put it somewhere else herself. Or—She wondered suddenly if Mr. Lemon could have been watching her this morning when she found the brass lid, and if he might have been interested in taking it himself. But that notion seemed absurd and she put it out of her mind. For the moment she had something more important to do.

When she reached her own bedroom she took the emerald star from the pocket of her shorts and put it away in a small box that held her best ring, a silver charm bracelet, and a gold locket that had been her grandmother's. It would be safe there until she could decide what to do about it. If she showed it to her mother, she knew what would happen. Mother would insist that she take it next door and give it to Mrs. Devery. But Julian had said, *Don't get her into any more trouble*—meaning Stella. Surely the star could stay here for a little while until she found a way to get it back to Stella.

When the box had been returned to its drawer and handkerchiefs piled over it, Robin stood before the dresser for a few moments studying the things that occupied its top, wondering what she might use as a subject for her clay piece. She picked up a small bronze elephant she used as a paperweight and looked at it carefully. But she did not want to copy something someone else had made.

She put the heavy thing down and went out on her private balcony, where she could look toward the Devery house. Through a gap in the trees she could see a small third-floor balcony rather like her own, outside the room in which Stella had been singing last night. Their rooms were close enough for them to call to each other, she thought. But Stella was not in sight and the door to her balcony was closed.

Robin could not put the other girl from her mind. What was it like to be blind? Had Stella ever been able to see—or had she been born blind? The feeling of pity was tight in her throat again and she had to swallow hard to make it go away. She wasn't sure she wanted to accept Julian's rather cold-seeming attitude. It seemed unkind not to be sorry for Stella.

She went inside and picked up a flowered babushka from the back of a chair. She folded it over and over until she had a long strip of material. This she tied firmly around her head, covering her eyes so that she could not see the faintest glimmer of light. It was a strange, bewildering feeling to think of herself as blind. It wasn't at all like playing the game of being blindfolded, because she was saying to herself, "I can't see at all. I am blind. For the rest of my life I won't be able to see."

The feeling was awful. She had lost her sense of direction and knew she was completely confused, right in her own bedroom. She did not know which way the door lay, or where the balcony was. She did not know which way to walk to find her bed, or dresser, or anything.

When Stella had crossed the lawn alone, she had not moved with her hands held out stiffly in front of her. But that was the way Robin moved now. She bumped her knee on a chair, but couldn't recall where she had last put this particular chair, so it gave her no location. She stumbled on with outstretched arms. With no consideration at all, the edge of the door, which she had been sure was closed came right between her reaching hands and bumped her hard on the nose.

"What in the world are you doing?" Tommy demanded from the hallway.

Blinking back tears from the blow, Robin snatched off the blindfold and stared at him angrily. "So it was you who opened the door? If I had run into it any harder, I'd probably have a nosebleed."

"How was I to know you were playing blindman's buff all by yourself?" Tommy asked.

"I was finding out what it's like to be blind," Robin said with dignity. "And anyway, you're supposed to knock when a door is closed."

"It was open part way," said Tommy. "You mean blind like that girl next door?"

So Tommy already knew. "Yes. And it was terrible. I couldn't even find my way around this room."

"Probably you have to learn how to be blind," Tommy said with considerable perception. "Stella doesn't go around looking as silly as you did. Anyway, Mom wants you downstairs right away. Stella's mother is here and I think there's trouble."

That would mean the star pin, Robin thought. What was going to happen? She paid no more attention to Tommy, but retrieved the star from its box and wrapped it in a handkerchief. Then she ran downstairs to the living room, where the pretty, black-haired woman she had seen last night was talking to Mother.

"Come in and sit down, Robin," her mother said. "This is Mrs. Dolores Devery from next door. She has been telling me something about a valuable emerald and diamond pin that you are supposed to have. What is this all about?"

Mother was dressed in the old clothes she used when she helped Dad in his painting. There was a smudge of green on her nose, her bronzy hair was coming out from under a scarf, and her glasses had slipped askew on the bridge of her nose. On her bare feet she wore thong sandals. Yet to look at her, sitting there so unselfconsciously, you'd have thought she was wearing her best dress. The Cuban woman looked far more upset than Mother did as she spoke in an apologetic voice to Robin.

"You have the star, yes? My Stella says she gives you this pin." She spoke English with an accent and a slight twisting of the order of the words.

"Here it is," Robin said, and unfolded her handkerchief to reveal the lovely star.

Mother gasped, a little less sure of herself. "Robin! How could you bring home a valuable thing like that without mentioning it to me?"

"I had to," Robin said. She explained to the young Mrs. Devery. "Stella's grandmother was angry with her and Stella didn't want her to know she was wearing the pin. I think she meant for me to hold it until her grandmother went back in the house. But then—"

Stella's mother nodded sadly as she took the pin. "Yes, I know. Stella tells to me all that has happened. I will give the pin to her and the grandmother does not know. It is better to return quickly now."

She stood up, clearly disturbed over being here, and worried lest the older Mrs. Devery should know of her visit. Mother tried to hold her for a moment longer, speaking to her in a friendly fashion.

"You've come here from Cuba, haven't you?"

The apologetic manner fell away, and young Mrs. Devery drew herself up very straight, her dark eyes flashing with a sudden fire.

"We belong to Free Cuba," she said. "My American husband died fighting for my country to be free."

Robin's mother reached out and touched the other woman's hand in silent sympathy. Tears came into Dolores Devery's eyes. She said a quick "thank you" to both Robin and her mother and hurried from the house as if old Mrs. Devery might be in angry pursuit. Dad, getting out of the car with a bag of groceries, passed her on the drive. The Cuban woman smiled at him fleetingly and hastened away.

"What was that all about?" Dad asked, as he carried the big paper bag into the house.

Robin and her mother followed him to the kitchen. Mother had a break in her voice as she explained what the Cuban woman had told them. But she lost it when she spoke of the pin.

"It seems," she informed Dad, "that our daughter calmly brought home a diamond and emerald pin, probably extremely valuable, and put it away in her room without a word to me."

Dad grinned. "At least she seems to have given it back. And I suppose she had a good reason for bringing it home."

"Of course I did!" Robin cried. "I was only trying to help the—" she managed to choke back the label

"blind" just in time—"help the girl next door. I didn't know what was going to happen. I didn't have time *not* to take the pin, even if I hadn't wanted to. I don't like that old Mrs. Devery."

"Tsk, tsk," said Mother, "prejudices, prejudices! I've been learning something of Agnes Devery from our neighbor, Mrs. Simpson. Stella's grandmother belongs to an old Staten Island family and she has lived right here in Catalpa Court all her life. In fact, Fred Devery, the man she married, grew up in that house that was torn down right across the street. Mrs. Simpson tells me that Edith Devery, his sister, was Agnes' best friend when they were young. Mrs. Devery has been terribly upset about the destruction of that house. Poor little Stella is blind, you know."

To her own surprise, Robin prickled as indignantly as Julian had, though she said nothing. If she were blind, she knew she would hate to be called "poor little Robin." To cool off, she went to the back door and stood looking up toward the corner room at the front of the Devery house. Julian was right. Pity was a looking down on someone less fortunate than yourself. It was quite different from sympathy.

From the kitchen Dad spoke to her gently. "How is this big project of yours coming along? Have you decided on the subject you want to model as an entry for Mr. Hornfeld's class?"

Robin knew she hadn't thought enough about it as yet. It wasn't that she had changed her mind, but that the strange happenings in the neighborhood had distracted her attention from the problem she needed most to think about. She shook her head vaguely and went out onto the back porch.

Her view of the upper corner of the Devery house wasn't as clear from below as it was from her own room, but through the leafy branches of maple trees she could glimpse Stella's balcony. As she looked up at it, the girl came out of her room and stood near the rail where a wide patch of sunlight fell through the leaves. As Robin watched, Stella raised her face to the warmth of the sun as if she drank it in through her very pores. Again the shock went through Robin. How dreadful if one couldn't see the sun.

Something sparkled on Stella's blouse and Robin saw that the star pin was back in place again. Emeralds on a cotton blouse! But she did not puzzle for long because it was the expression on Stella's face that held her attention. Her cleft chin looked rounded and soft, her mouth was curved in a secret smile, as if her thoughts amused her and were not at all unpleasant.

Once more Robin had the feeling of catching her breath—as she had when Stella had first smiled at Julian Hornfeld. There was something wonderful about the way she looked. Something that would surely make any artist long to catch her likeness on paper. Or make a sculptor want to . . . Why of course!

She dashed back to the kitchen, where Mother stood on a stepladder, putting groceries away and Dad admired his handiwork on painted cupboards.

"I've decided!" Robin cried. "I know what I want to model. I'm going to do a head of Stella Devery!"

There was a stunned silence in the kitchen. Mother edged about on the stepladder with three cans of soup in her hands, and Dad turned his back on painted shelves.

"Oh, no!" Mother said softly. "Robin dear, you mustn't try something as difficult as a likeness. You mustn't doom yourself to failure before you start. Even a figure is easier to do than a portrait head. Or you could make a vase, or some sort of animal—almost anything but this."

Robin closed her eyes and tried to shut out the sound of her mother's words. She knew very well her mother was right, yet in her mind's eye she could catch glimpse after glimpse of Stella Devery's fascinating face. If it was there so clearly in her imagination, surely she could transfer it into clay. At least she had to try.

Dad's deep-blue eyes were sympathetic. "Isn't it better to take things a step at a time when you're only beginning? There can be a pretty big disappointment in reaching so far beyond your present capability."

She knew they were both talking sensibly, but she didn't want to listen. A marvelous dream glimmered in her mind. It possessed as shining a radiance as Stella's pin catching the sun. Her fingers ached with longing to capture this beauty and mold it into clay.

"I have to do it," she said. "I have to try."

"Then there's nothing more to be said," Dad told her. "If you must hitch your wagon to a star, go ahead. But there's not much time to reach that star."

Mother set the soup cans on the shelf with three separate thumps. "It's not practical," she said over her shoulder. "Mrs. Devery isn't friendly toward newcomers. How are you going to model Stella's head without any Stella to sit for you?"

"When I close my eyes I can see everything about her," Robin said dreamily, and closed her eyes. Abruptly there was nothing there to be seen. The magical dream had vanished without a trace. She could remember only vaguely how Stella looked. This did not worry her, because the vision would return when she saw Stella again. She opened her eyes and smiled at her mother. "You'll help me," she said. "I know you can find a way."

Dad chuckled. "A sound approach, honey. And I'll bet it works."

"Flattery will get you nowhere," said Mother, and went back to work on the shelves.

Dad winked at Robin, and Robin winked back at him. If Mother took it into her head to help—even if she didn't think much of the project—she would never give up. A way would be found for Stella to be seen as frequently as was necessary for Robin to see her. And that was a wonderful prospect. She wanted to know Stella better, as well as to model her face.

Before Mother could think up any new objections, Robin slipped out of the kitchen and went skipping around the backyard with Herr Binglebaum at her heels. Tommy, concentrating deeply, paid no attention to this outburst of exuberance. When Robin had exhausted some of her urge to blow off steam, she paused to look up again at the Devery house.

Stella was gone from her balcony, but in the moment Robin's eyes moved upward, she caught a flicker of something at another window. It was no more than a glimpse and it vanished from the corner of her eye as she turned her full gaze upon the window where she had seen it. Yet something had been there—something like a round moon face looking down at her.

Had Mr. Lemon, as he called himself, somehow managed to get inside the Devery house? The thought was not a pleasant one and it put a damper on Robin's new excitement over her plan for the coming weeks.

It was time to tell someone about what had happened last night, about the disappearance of the brass lid, and about the glimpse of a face she had seen at a Devery window. There was only one person who would not laugh at her—Julian Hornfeld.

Robin slipped away from Balmy and walked out to the front sidewalk.

(6)

Robin Tells Her Story

ROBIN FOLLOWED the curve of the oval toward the Hornfeld house, but Julian was nowhere in sight. Mr. Hornfeld was in the front garden, talking to his wife as she knelt beside a rose bed. The Hornfelds did not confine themselves to a plain front lawn. They had attractive flower beds, with something constantly in bloom.

Mrs. Hornfeld smiled at Robin. She was slightly plump and she had the good sense not to put herself into slacks or shorts. Her face was round and pretty, with an attractive touch of pink in her cheeks. Her softly graying hair made a curly fluff around her face, and her blue eyes were always friendly. There was something reassuringly serene about Mrs. Hornfeld. Robin had the feeling that no matter whether her children misbehaved, or her artistic husband turned temperamental, she would always be good-natured and relaxed. Robin felt much less shy with her than with Julian's father, and she spoke to her now, not looking at the sculptor.

"Is Julian around, do you think?"

Before Mrs. Hornfeld could answer, her husband said, "Julian's out in back. At the moment he's busy not being a juvenile delinquent."

Robin stared at him blankly.

Mrs. Hornfeld's eyes were twinkling. "What Ira means is that Julian is cleaning his father's studio."

"Exactly," said the sculptor, his neatly pointed gray beard giving emphasis as he nodded his head. "America became a strong country because of the men and women who worked to make it strong. What teen-agers need aren't more playgrounds and more amusements. They need good, sound, important work that must be done. Julian's mother has enough to do and I can't work in an untidy room. So cleaning my studio is important and Julian knows it."

"Go right through the house," Mrs. Hornfeld said to Robin. "Don't lecture her, Ira."

Robin ducked around the formidable figure of Mr. Hornfeld and went up the steps and through the unhooked screen door. Two little girls were playing house in the front hall, and they regarded Robin gravely as she went past. She remembered that the studio was in a frame building that must once have been a carriage house. Mr. Hornfeld had taken out the stalls and partitions, put in a raised wooden floor and several extra windows, so that he had a large, well-lighted studio in which to work. There was space for even his largest marble and stone pieces.

Through the screen door Robin could see Julian busily shoving around a large push broom. "Hi!" she called. "Do you care if I come in?"

He beckoned her in cheerfully, and she was delighted to step into the studio again. When she had seen it the first time, the place had been filled with grown-ups, and she had not been able to wander around by herself. There was so much to see. On wall shelves were all sorts of finished pieces of a small size. On separate work pedestals set on casters so they could easily be moved and turned were figures of marble and stone and terra-cotta. There were some fascinating wood carvings.

Robin sniffed the air with satisfaction. She liked the smell of the studio—a smell of damp clay, of stone, of wood dust. Pausing before a shelf of somewhat less expert work, she looked at it curiously. Julian pushed his broom in her direction.

"Some of Dad's younger students have done those pieces." He glanced at her with interest. "Your brother, Tommy, says you'd like to enter Dad's class. If you make it, you'll have a piece up there too. That's his requirement, you know. You have to submit something he approves. Then it sits on that shelf until you do something better."

Robin took a deep breath. "I'm going to work on a clay head. I'm going to try my best to submit something good enough to go up there. I've got something in mind, but please don't tell your father yet."

Julian pushed a pile of stone chips and bits of dry clay and slivers of wood toward a dustpan and leaned over to shovel it in. "I won't tell him. What are you going to try?"

Robin almost wished he had not asked, wished she had not spoken. In a way she wanted to tell him, yet at the same time she hesitated. If Julian reacted the way her parents had, perhaps she would feel discouraged before she started, and she could not afford to have that happen. Trying not to be fearful, she blurted out the truth.

"I'm going to do a head of Stella Devery. If I can."

Julian whistled a long, soft note, but he did not laugh. "That will be tough, but I don't blame you for wanting to try. The other day I was attempting to get her down on paper. In words, I mean. I didn't have much luck, but I think I'll keep trying."

"That's what I mean to do," Robin said. "I don't expect to get anything right the first time."

"You won't," said Julian frankly. "You'll need to know what she's like first. Then something that won't be just an outward copy will come through."

Robin hadn't thought of that. She spoke on the spur of the moment. "Tell me about her."

Julian went on with his work and she saw that he was doing a careful clean-up job. He wasn't hurrying or skimping at the task. Clearly he was a workman who took pride in whatever he did.

"Tell you what about her?" he asked after a long silence.

Again she spoke impetuously. "I don't know—maybe about the party and why she slapped you."

Julian threw her a startled look, but he did not seem to be offended. He was willing to explain, now that she knew Stella was blind.

"It was Mother's idea to get Mrs. Simpson to invite Stella to Mary Lou's party, even though Stella is twelve. Mother thought she ought to get out from behind those hedges and meet some of the children in the neighborhood. Mother meant to be there herself, to keep an eye on things and help make it easier for Stella. But my youngest sister got sick and Mother couldn't go. So she sent me."

Julian worked busily with his broom for a minute, and Robin moved from sculpture to sculpture, waiting for him to continue.

"It's not that I'm so bad at kid parties," Julian said.

"I'm used to younger children at home. But I didn't know what to do about Stella. I can imagine how awful a blind person must feel when there's noise and confusion all around, with people running and yelling. It must be upsetting and maybe a little scary. I think Stella got scared and I don't blame her. Mrs. Simpson put her in a corner chair and she sat there and wouldn't come out."

"She wore that pin on her dress, didn't she?" Robin asked.

Julian nodded. "Mrs. Simpson didn't approve of that, and she kept staring at it. Anyway, after a while Mary Lou and the other kids began to play 'pin the tail on the donkey.' Mrs. Simpson would tie on a blindfold, spin the child around, and send him off with a tail to pin on. You remember. I got the idea that this might be a game Stella would be wonderful at."

The red tinge was creeping into his cheeks again, and he did not look at Robin as he worked.

"I pulled her out of her chair and told her I'd take her over and show her where the donkey picture was. I told her she could win the prize easily and she wouldn't need a blindfold. But that girl can go off like a firecracker! Somehow she got the notion that I was making fun of her. I guess she thought that because it was a game where people had to pretend to be blind, we were ridiculing her. When I got her as far as the middle of the floor all the noise stopped because everyone was watching. That must have been scary too—when she couldn't tell what anyone was doing, or where they were. She wanted me to take her back to her corner, but I thought she ought to try at least, and I wouldn't. That's when she slapped me—good and hard. She knew right where to aim because I was talking to her. Afterward she started to cry and Mrs. Simpson rushed over to tell her she was a poor, dear unfortunate little girl—and I was an awfully mean boy. That made Stella cry harder than ever. Why wouldn't she? Everyone was treating her like a baby, so she acted like a baby."

"How perfectly awful!" Robin said.

Julian agreed. "It was. If Mother had been there, it wouldn't have happened. Anyway, Mrs. Simpson had to take Stella home because she was getting hysterical. I went along, even though they didn't want me, because I felt responsible. So I saw what happened when Mrs. Devery came out on the veranda, and Mrs. Simpson told her what had happened. The old lady was furious. She hadn't wanted Stella to go in the first place. And she was madder than ever when she saw that valuable pin her granddaughter was wearing on her dress." Julian broke off, looking thoroughly miserable.

It must have been dreadful to be caught in such an unpleasant affair, when he had only meant to help, Robin thought.

He dumped another dustpan of debris into a trash can and grinned at her unexpectedly.

"You'd never guess what happened when Mrs. Devery started to bawl me out. Stella stopped crying and told her grandmother that what had happened was her fault, not mine. She said I had been kinder to her than anybody else and she was sorry she had slapped me."

Somehow Robin was not surprised. She had already seen Stella show a rebellious and contrary spirit in the face of her grandmother's disapproval.

"Good for her!" Robin said. "What did Mrs. Devery do then?"

Julian made a face. "She said a lady never slapped anyone, no matter what the provocation. And she said of course she should not have allowed Stella to go to the party with those rough children who didn't know they had to be careful with a blind child. I thought Stella was going to shoot off fireworks all over again, but her mother came home from her job just then. She helps to take care of Spanish-speaking children over in town while their mothers work. Young Mrs. Devery is a gentle person and I think she's afraid of her mother-in-law, but she did the neatest job I ever saw of getting Stella out of her grandmother's hands and upstairs where she could calm down. That evening she came to our house to thank me for being kind to Stella."

Julian's forehead was damp with perspiration as he relived the experience in telling about it. Robin's eyes glowed as he finished, not only because she admired Julian but because of Stella too, and her Cuban mother, who was a stranger here and had a difficult problem to solve if they must live with old Mrs. Devery.

"Do you know when Stella became blind?" Robin asked.

"She was born that way. She doesn't have any memory of sight. That makes her life different from ours in so many ways. Blind people who can remember sight are in a more fortunate position. For instance, how can you imagine the sky if you've never seen the sky? How can you tell a person who has never seen a color what blue is like?"

"Perhaps that's not so important," said a voice behind them.

Robin turned to see that Mr. Hornfeld had come into the studio.

"It seems to me," he went on, "that the most important thing for a blind person to learn is how to live with his own four senses and make good use of them in the world of his own experience. Things like the sky and what a color is like belong to a make-believe world for a person who was born blind. Stella has to accept such things and believe in them—and then work hard at gathering her own much more real experiences."

"But how can anyone believe in what he can't imagine?" Robin asked hesitantly.

Mr. Hornfeld's smile was like Julian's. There was kindness in it and she stopped feeling quite so shy with him.

He went to a clay model and took off the damp cloths that kept the clay moist and workable. "Would you like to see something I'm working on?"

Robin came eagerly to view the head. The sculptor turned the stand on its casters and she saw the grave beauty, the sadness, the supreme understanding in the face that looked out from the clay. Ira Hornfeld was modeling a head of Jesus.

"How wonderful!" said Robin softly.

"This is one of a series I'm doing," Mr. Hornfeld explained. "There's Moses over there."

He waved one hand at another head and Robin saw a wise, strong, bearded face gleaming in finished bronze.

"I have still to do Mohammed and Buddha," he continued. "I shall call the series 'Men of Faith.' This has a bearing on what we were talking about. You understand, don't you, that there is one face I can never find in the clay?"

Robin wasn't sure what he meant, and she said nothing.

"Can you tell me what God is like?" Mr. Hornfeld asked.

Julian was watching, smiling a little because he understood what his father was getting at. Robin shook her head.

"But you do believe in God?"

"Of course," Robin said.

"That is the right answer," Mr. Hornfeld told her gravely. "Although this is a name that man has given to something he can never know or fully understand. It's not for us here on earth to comprehend. We can see God only with the eyes of our spirit. We have only to look at the living world around us to accept something that is beyond our ability to understand."

Robin listened, her eyes brightening as his meaning came clear. "The way Stella has to accept the sky and the colors of the rainbow, though she has never seen them. Is that what you mean?"

"I'm pleased with you," said Ira Hornfeld, and Robin flushed with pleasure, right to her ears. "That is exactly what I mean. Our young friend Stella need not let her inability to visualize spoil the rest of living, any more than our lack of knowledge about God needs to make us any the less thankful for the world he has created."

There was a silence and Mr. Hornfeld turned to his son.

"I want to get back to work now. Let the rest of the cleaning go for the present."

Julian handed the dustpan to Robin and picked up the trash can and broom. They left the studio quietly, not speaking until they were outside.

"I think your father is wonderful," Robin said, the spell of Mr. Hornfeld's voice and words still upon her. "Just the same, he scares me a little."

Julian set the cleaning things down near the garage door. "He scares me too. Mainly because he won't ever accept anything second-rate. I'm not always up to what he expects of me. But maybe it's good to have a goal you can't quite reach."

Robin thought uneasily of the head of Stella that was still only a vision in her mind. To meet Mr. Hornfeld's standards was going to be more difficult than she had expected. But still, she had to try. Now that the spell of the studio and the thoughts it provoked had been lifted, she suddenly remembered what she had come here to tell Julian.

"Could I talk to you a minute?" she asked.

"Sure," he said. "Let's get into the shade."

As the morning wore on, the sun had grown increasingly hot in a blazing, cloudless blue sky. Julian led the way to a big hydrangea bush in the backyard. They sat down close to the small rim of cool shade it offered at this hour, and Robin looked up at blossoms that had once been a pinky blue, and were fading to rust as they shed their petals on the ground. How terrible it would be never to have seen a flower, she thought—and then remembered Mr. Hornfeld's comforting words. Stella still had four good senses through which she could experience the world. She reached up through broad green leaves and cupped her hand lightly about a rusty blossom. Here was a sense knowledge of hydrangeas that she, who could see, had never experienced before.

But Julian was waiting and she began to tell him of the mysterious happenings that had involved Mrs. Devery last night, and of the way the man who called himself Mr. Lemon had watched her so secretly and run away when Balmy discovered him. She told how Mrs. Devery had found something in the rubble, and how

Robin had picked up the brass lid this morning—only to have it disappear so strangely. Finally she told him of the face she had seen looking down at her from an upper window of the Devery house—a face she felt sure was Mr. Lemon's.

Julian heard her through and he did not jeer or tell her she was probably mistaken. He seemed to believe in what she related and though he asked a question or two, they were not challenging questions that doubted her word or her judgment.

"It sounds pretty strange," he admitted when she had told him all she knew. "I've seen this fellow around Catalpa Court for a day or two and I've been wondering what he was about. But I didn't talk to him until this morning."

"Do you think he could have gone inside the Devery house without anyone knowing?" Robin asked.

Julian pondered this. "I suppose it's possible. But since this is Saturday, Stella's mother is home, as well as her grandmother. And there's Flora too. Flora does the cooking for them and helps with the housework. She's worked there for a long time and she's very responsible. I'm sure she'd know if anyone sneaked into the house. Of course Flora goes home nights after dinner. Anyway, let's keep our eyes open and see what happens next."

They left it at that and Robin went thoughtfully home. At the Ward house her mother was bidding Mrs. Simpson good-by at the front door. When Mary Lou's mother had gone, she gave her daughter a triumphant, everything-is-settled smile.

"It's all arranged," she said. "You and I are going to call on Mrs. Devery tomorrow afternoon. The old lady doesn't know what we want, but she says we may come over. Mrs. Simpson belongs to one of the old families too, though she's in a younger generation. She understands what we want to accomplish, so she has fixed everything up on the phone with Mrs. Devery."

Robin could only regard her mother in astonished admiration. "What do we want to accomplish?" she asked, since her mother was going a bit too fast for her to keep up.

Mrs. Ward ran a hand through her already mussed hair and headed back to her work. "Why, to have Stella Devery come over here every morning for sittings," she said over her shoulder. "And perhaps to have fun working in clay herself."

Robin ran after her mother. "But do you think Mrs. Devery will let her do that? Julian says she doesn't like Stella to go outside her own grounds."

"We'll have to see," Mother said. "And now, my growing daughter, how would you like to run upstairs and dust the library thoroughly? You've been slipping up on your chores for the last couple of days."

Robin gave her mother an affectionate smile. She was wonderful. If anyone could break old Mrs. Devery down, Mother could.

"Sure, I'll dust," Robin said. "Right away. After all, I don't want to turn into a juvenile delinquent."

Mother whirled to look at her, but Robin only laughed and ran upstairs without explaining Mr. Hornfeld's interesting philosophy.

(7)

The Brass Lid Turns Up

THE NEXT MORNING Robin was witness to a surprising emergence from the Devery house. She had dressed for church in her best green frock and a white piqué hat. Her white socks were spotlessly clean, and she had managed not to scrape her ankles together or get grass stains on her white shoes.

The Staten Island breeze had failed them for once, and the leaves on the trees hung limp in the humid August heat. Robin stood beside the birdbath, having taken another careful look around to see if she could locate the missing brass lid. Dad had gone to get the car out of the garage and Tommy had disappeared in his own peculiar way, as he usually did when the family was about to go anywhere. Mother was still upstairs.

Although Robin could not see the Devery veranda, the click of high heels was audible as someone walked across it. At once Robin darted toward the gap in the hedge. The hole had not been patched up as yet. Instead, it had somehow grown a bit larger, so that it was now easier to look through into the Devery garden without getting down on one's hands and knees.

Mrs. Dolores Devery, wearing a beige cotton suit and red shoes with very high heels, was coming down the steps with Stella holding on to her arm. Stella wore her fluffy white dress, and both she and her mother had on summer hats and white gloves. They walked easily together. Mrs. Devery did not hurry, but neither did she move slowly. Stella's hand was in the crook of her mother's elbow and she did not falter.

When they reached the gate, Robin left the hedge and stationed herself where the two would pass her as they came by. A thought had suddenly occurred to her. There was no time to check with Dad, but she was sure he wouldn't mind. When Stella and her mother drew near, Robin spoke to them politely.

"Good morning. If you're on your way to church, maybe we could give you a lift? We're leaving in a little while."

Mrs. Devery glanced doubtfully at Robin, then back at the dark towers that showed above the hedges. Stella turned her face in the direction of Robin's voice, but today she did not smile.

"Thank you very much," Stella's mother said. "But perhaps it is better"— again the anxious glance over her shoulder—"better if we hurry to catch our bus. We are going down the hill and over to St. Peter's. Perhaps this is not on your way?"

Dad heard them talking and came out to add his own invitation. "We'll be happy to drop you off if you can wait a few minutes. It's not out of our way at all."

The sound of garage doors being opened in the Devery house reached the group on the sidewalk, and at once Mrs. Devery appeared anxious to be on her way. She smiled apologetically at Mother, who had joined them, and murmured that they were grateful, but they must hurry in order to catch the bus. It was not necessary to trouble them.

The fact was plain that she wanted no encounter with Agnes Devery at the moment. There was nothing to do but let them go.

Mother tapped her toe on the sidewalk and spoke to Dad. "Mrs. Simpson tells me that old Mrs. Devery had a fit when her only son went off to Cuba. And she had a double fit when he married a Cuban woman who is a Catholic. Apparently she still thinks her own four walls are all of the world that counts. I'd like to give that woman a piece of my mind."

Robin looked at her in alarm. "Oh, Mother—if you do, she'll never let Stella come and model for me."

"Your mother's letting off steam," Dad said. "Now if we can manage to locate our only son, perhaps we can get along to church ourselves."

While Mother was calling Tommy, old Mrs. Devery came out of her driveway in an ancient black Buick, holding onto the wheel as though it were attached to bucking horses that might get away from her at any moment. Her face was dark as a thundercloud, and she drove toward the street without glancing at the Wards.

Mother looked after her in a speculating manner. "I suspect she wouldn't drive her daughter-in-law to a Catholic church, and Mrs. Devery didn't want to be found getting a lift from the neighbors."

Poor Stella, Robin thought, living in a house where only certain labels could be approved. If Mrs. Devery hated words like "Jew" and "Cuban" and "Catholic," she probably had still more labels that would make living difficult for herself and those around her. "Newcomer" was undoubtedly one of them.

"Let's get into the car," Dad said. "Since our son Thomas is not around, we'll leave him at home. It's getting late."

Of course Tommy showed up in the nick of time, as he always did. His reddish hair was mussed and he had managed to get a streak of dirt across his snub nose, but at least his gray suit was still clean, and his grin announced confidently that he was never really late for anything.

While Dad backed the car out and Mother rubbed at Tommy's nose with a clean handkerchief, Robin glanced at the high towers of the Devery house that were visible above hedge and wall. As she looked, her eyes widened. The face was there again in an upper window.

It was Mr. Lemon, and he was looking out over the Devery garden as boldly as though he owned the place. Once more Robin's heart began to thump in her chest. She had the feeling that Mr. Lemon's presence in the Devery house was somehow wrong. It seemed impossible that old Mrs. Devery, who disliked anyone who did not belong to her own small circle, should actually invite a person like Mr. Lemon into her home. Yet there he was, and this time he did not trouble to duck out of sight.

There was no solving the problem now and when Dad called, Robin got into the car beside Tommy.

More than once that morning Robin found herself looking around the church, almost afraid to find that Mrs. Devery might belong to the same congregation. But she seemed to worship elsewhere, and Robin could not help feeling relieved.

For Robin, the day passed slowly until midafternoon when she and her mother were due at Mrs. Devery's. Except for hats, they put on the same clothes they had worn to church, and Robin was pleased over that. She could never be sure what Mother might choose to do. She could suddenly turn independent, put on her oldest clothes, and announce that if people didn't like her for herself and as she was—well, then, never mind! This was an attitude Robin did not approve of, and she was glad Mother was going to be proper today and behave like other people who went visiting on Sunday.

The Devery gate was not locked during the day and they could walk right in. The moment they started across the lawn Robin saw Stella. The girl was in blue jeans again—perhaps she did not know that company was coming. She sat on a square of brown blanket in the shade of an enormously tall blue spruce tree. Her hands were clasped about her knees, and her face was raised toward the tree, her eyes closed.

Mother called out to her. "This is Mrs. Ward, and Robin is with me. We've come to call on your grandmother."

Stella did a strange thing. She did not answer the greeting, even when Robin added her own "Hello." Instead, she rolled off the blanket, then picked it up and put it over her head, covering herself completely as if she were sitting under a tent.

Somehow the action seemed shocking. It was the sort of thing a young child who knew no manners might do. But from a girl of twelve it was startling and rude. Robin looked at her mother, both worried and puzzled. Mother raised her shoulders slightly to indicate that she did not understand either.

Together they climbed broad wooden steps, some of which sagged a little from age, and crossed the unscreened front veranda which continued around one side of the house. The big front door was closed and two oval panes of glass set into the upper panels were frosted, so that one could not see into the front hall. Only the tinkling of glass wind-bells, stirred by the faint breath of their passing, sounded in the hot silence.

This must have been Flora's day off, for Mrs. Devery herself came to answer their ring. She wore a thin dress of dark gray silk with a hem that fell to an unfashionable length above old-fashioned oxford shoes. She greeted them without warmth and showed them into what must once have been a vast drawing room running from the front to the back of the house. The rear half of the room was partitioned off by sliding wooden doors, which were partially closed, making the space smaller. Robin could see that the furniture beyond wore dust covers and the blinds were tightly drawn.

This front part of the room, dim and curtained, seemed at first much cooler than the outdoors. But because the windows were closed, the air soon seemed stuffy and stale, like air that had been left over from bygone years. Mrs. Devery touched an electric switch and a magnificent crystal chandelier came to life and shed its radiance over the room.

Robin saw that the furniture was as beautiful as anything she had seen in a museum. Indeed, because of past museum visits, she knew that the sofa with its faded-green damask and high curving back was made of fine rosewood.

Mrs. Devery invited them to sit down, and took a chair beside a marble fireplace. On the mantel above, an ornate gilt clock gave out a dignified ticking. Mother seated herself comfortably and began to chat pleasantly about how much she liked Catalpa Court and Staten Island. Robin perched on the edge of the sofa, and stole secret looks about the room.

Mrs. Devery listened to Mother without interest, clearly waiting for them to state the purpose of their visit and leave. She was not going to make things easy for them, even if Mrs. Simpson had arranged this call.

Except for Mother's light, cheerful voice and the solemn ticking of the clock, the house seemed quiet. Robin could hear no footsteps moving about upstairs, though she listened for them. If Mr. Lemon was still here, he kept himself well out of sight.

At first the brilliant light from the chandelier had dazzled Robin's eyes, but now, studying the handsome marble fireplace and mantel, she noticed the full-length portrait that hung on the wall above. The young woman in the painting wore a pale-yellow gown. Her thick brown hair was brushed upward in a pompadour, and her slender hands held a book on her lap. She sat in a rosewood chair beside a marble fireplace, and suddenly Robin recognized that life had repeated the pose in the portrait. Surely this was the same chair in which Mrs. Devery now sat before the very same fireplace.

Her attention quickening, Robin studied the lovely young face in the picture—and was startled into recognition. It was Stella's face—almost. The girl in the picture was older, of course, yet the beautiful mouth was nearly the same. The eyes of the picture were blue, whereas Stella's were hazel. The nose was quite different—but something else was the same. At times there was a willful look about Stella—and this girl wore the same expression. It seemed to Robin that the picture was of someone who would not do exactly as you expected, who was likely to fly in the face of those who opposed her.

The resemblance was so surprising that Robin exclaimed aloud about it. "That picture could have been

painted of Stella!" she cried. "If Stella were older . . .
Has Stella a sister?" she asked Mrs. Devery.

Mother's eyes moved to the painting. Mrs. Devery
did not trouble to look upward. Instead she turned her
cold regard upon Robin.

"That portrait was painted of me when I was eighteen
years old and first came to this house as a bride. I do not
believe it looks in the least like my granddaughter."

It was the second time that day Robin had blushed to
her very ears. How stupid could she be! Why hadn't
she guessed at once the identity of the girl in the picture?
Of course there was a resemblance to the woman she
had grown into, but the older version was far less flat-
tering and Robin had not seen the likeness. How dreadful to have one's face harden into resentment lines, hate
lines, when once it had been so beautiful—especially
since this was something Mrs. Devery had done to herself. No one else was responsible for such marks on her
face.

"You had a request to make of me, I believe?" Mrs.
Devery said to Mrs. Ward.

Mother threw her daughter a look of reproach which
Robin understood. This matter of the portrait had not
endeared her visitors to Mrs. Devery. Nevertheless,
Mother plunged ahead, trying to make use of the chance
that had been offered her.

"Just as that painter must have been eager to do your
portrait, my daughter is anxious to model a head of
your granddaughter. We are wondering if—"

"My portrait," Mrs. Devery broke in, "was done by
one of the distinguished portrait painters of the time.
A man who happened to live on Staten Island."

"Of course," Mother rushed on. "And Robin is only

a young girl and very much a beginner. Yet the same quality is there in Stella's face and she has seen it. We thought you might be willing to let your granddaughter come next door for an hour or two every morning to pose for Robin. Perhaps nothing will come of the effort, but Robin wants so much to try. And Stella might enjoy working in clay too."

"My granddaughter is blind," said Mrs. Devery, her voice cold and flat. She might as well have said, My granddaughter is helpless and hopeless.

Robin's mother answered in her gentlest voice. "Your granddaughter has hands. Slender, sensitive hands, like those of the girl in that picture. She doesn't need eyes to use them well."

Mrs. Devery moved her own hands in her lap and Robin looked at them for the first time. They were wrinkled and blue-veined. Several rings weighed them down, yet they were still long and slender like those of the girl Mrs. Devery had once been.

"Perhaps we should ask Stella's mother," Mrs. Ward said, suddenly bright and cheerful, knowing perfectly well that she was waving a red flag at Mrs. Devery. Robin almost grinned.

"*I* make the decisions in this house," said Mrs. Devery. "The child's mother is a stranger in this country. She knows nothing about such matters. In any event, the idea is impossible because Stella herself would not consent to this. She does not enjoy the company of those who do not understand what being blind is like. You saw what she did when you came up the walk—the way she hid under her blanket."

So Mrs. Devery had been watching, Robin thought. She could see that the visit was about to come to an end and that Mrs. Devery had decided against their request. All Robin's plans were to be swept aside by those thin fingers. She jumped eagerly to her feet.

"I'll ask Stella myself!" she cried. "Mother, wait right here while I go and ask her."

There was no time for Mrs. Devery to speak, to object, to halt this abrupt flight. A moment later Robin was out on the veranda.

Stella had come from beneath the stifling blanket and was lying on her back on the grass, an arm of the blue spruce reaching over her. No star pin twinkled on her blouse today. Robin ran toward her across the lawn, not calling until she had nearly reached her. Then she said, "It's only Robin, from next door," and put a quick foot on the blanket before Stella could reach out and catch it up. When she tried, Robin sat down on it, cross-legged, so that Stella could not tip her off.

"Don't hide from me," Robin pleaded. "I want to tell you something, ask you something. I need your help. I need it terribly!"

The guarded look on Stella's face gave way to astonishment, but before she could speak Robin rushed on. She told the other girl about Julian's father and his studio and about how much she wanted to be in his class. She explained how Mr. Hornfeld made the rule that a piece of work must be submitted to him and later judged along with other pieces, so that the most promising young people could enter his special class. By the time she got to the point—that it was Stella's face she wanted to model—her words were tumbling one over another in her eagerness to convince and persuade. When she finished, she was not sure whether she had made any sense at all.

Nevertheless, a new alertness had come to life in Stella. At least she was curious.

"Why did you choose me?" she asked.

"I don't know, exactly," Robin said. "There's something about the way you look that I want to put into clay. If I can."

"I don't know if I believe you," Stella said. "Lots of times blind people don't express much in their faces. My father said that children who can see copy the expressions on other people's faces, while children who have never been able to see may not know how to do this."

"You know how," said Robin earnestly.

"That's because my father made me work at it. He said my mother's face was one of the most expressive he'd ever seen and sometimes he used to make me touch the lines of her face and try to imitate them. So perhaps I do it without thinking. Except when I don't want to give away my feelings."

"Like now?" Robin said.

Stella was silent for a moment. "Maybe you only want to use me because I'm blind—because I'm queer and different," she said at last.

Robin shook her head emphatically and then remembered that Stella could not see the gesture. She reached out and clasped the other girl by the wrist, as though she might make her understand by the pressure of her fingers. For an instant Stella's hand stiffened beneath Robin's, but she did not draw away.

"I don't think it has anything to do with your being blind," Robin said. "You don't look blind at all. Your eyes are beautiful."

Stella jerked her hand away. "I can make you squirm if I tell you something. I can give you shivers. Shall I try?"

Robin blinked, not knowing what was to come.

"I *will* tell you," Stella said.

This time it was she who reached toward Robin and laid a hand on her arm, as if she meant to read any quiver of reaction through her sense of touch.

"My eyes were ugly and deformed," Stella said. "I used to squinch them closed all the time. Then I had an operation and they put in plastic eyes. How do you like that?"

Robin held her arm still beneath the other girl's touch. She could feel a slight uneasiness start at the pit of her stomach and she drew a deep, quiet breath and swallowed hard. Because the idea of plastic eyes was new to her, she did feel a little shocked. But Stella must not be allowed to guess that this was true.

"My grandmother has false teeth and they don't shock me," Robin said, hoping her voice sounded right.

Stella waited, not lifting her hand.

"Once I knew a man with an artificial leg and that didn't shock me," said Robin, warming to her subject. "A good many people wear hearing aids and glasses, and no one minds." The faint squirminess had been forced back and she was safe again. "I think it's wonderful that you look the way you do. The color of your eyes is so natural that no one would ever guess if you didn't tell. Just the same, I don't think I'd care even if you still squinched up your eyes."

"I'll pose for you," Stella said abruptly and lifted her hand. "Perhaps when you catch whatever you see in the clay, I can see it too—with my fingers."

"Will your grandmother let you come to our house?" Robin asked.

Stella made a face. "Let's go and find out."

She stood up and Robin rose beside her.

"I came outside because I don't like to stay in the house right now," Stella said. "Not since that man with the lemon drops moved in."

"Who is he?" Robin asked, quickly alert.

"I don't know. Grandmother hasn't mentioned him. I think they keep him out of my mother's way too. But because I'm blind, they think I can't tell he's around. That's how stupid they are!"

"I've seen him," Robin admitted. "I don't like him either."

"I can hear him creaking about the house," Stella went on. "This morning I found a packet of sticky lemon drops he left in the dining room. I know he watches me. That's why I brought my blanket outside—to hide under it if he came around. I don't like to be stared at when I don't know who is staring, or from where."

"You didn't need to hide from us," Robin said.

Stella's smile was suddenly friendly. "I know that now."

She raised her head, listening. The air was hot and still and there was no sound of wind-bells to give her a direction. She reached for Robin's arm and her touch was light and sure as they started toward the house together.

At first Robin moved hesitantly, but she found that Stella walked normally and that she sensed at once any turn Robin might make. When Robin slowed, Stella knew they had reached the front steps, and she felt for the first one with her toe, almost without seeming to. She knew the number of steps and did not fumble at the top. Before they entered the house, she spoke to Robin.

"Thanks for not pushing or pulling me, the way my grandmother does. Grandmother always acts as if—" she chuckled softly, "as if I were blind!"

That Stella could make a joke about blindness was somehow both surprising and reassuring. It made Robin feel more comfortable with her, and she laughed too.

Stella heard and was pleased. "You're not afraid of me," she said with satisfaction. "Sometimes people are, you know. Older people, as well as young. They shout as if I were deaf, or they think I must be stupid because I can't see. Sometimes they keep away from me as if blindness were some sort of disease they might catch. But the worst thing of all is when they ooze pity because they're so, so sorry for me."

Her voice had grown suddenly sharp and she paused with her hand on the china knob of the front door.

"Are *you* sorry for me, Robin Ward?"

Again Robin laughed. "I was in the beginning— when I didn't know any better. Julian scolded me and I got over it right away."

"That's fine," Stella said. "A real friend isn't someone who is sorry for you. I hate people who drool because I'm a poor little blind girl. Or the others who act as if I were a genius because I can walk across a room by myself. They're the ones who think about blindness all the time. And that's silly, because I don't. Or anyway, I wouldn't if they didn't push it at me so much."

Robin followed her into the hall, feeling that she was learning a great deal every moment she was with Stella. These things would have to be taken out and thought about later so they could be digested and fully understood. She wasn't nearly as clever about blindness as Stella thought. Perhaps Stella expected too much of sighted people. They had such a lot to learn about blindness.

Once the two girls were in the gloomy hall that stretched from the front of the house to the back, with a still darker stairway running upward on the lefthand side, Stella was more sure of herself than Robin.

For someone with sight, the sudden change from bright sunlight to this dim interior was confusing and eerie. In that moment, while Robin was the blind one, she heard a sound at the head of the stairs.

Stella nudged her and whispered, "He's up there now, snooping."

Robin shivered as she followed Stella into the drawing room. The fat little man with the lemon drops was all wrong for the villain of a mystery, yet she felt he was exactly that. Whatever he was up to wasn't anything good, she was sure.

In the drawing room Stella went at once to a straight chair near a window and stood behind it, her hands resting on the back. That way, Robin sensed, she knew exactly where she was.

Mrs. Ward's cheeks were pink in the light from the chandelier, and Mrs. Devery was looking both superior and disagreeable. Clearly the conversation had not been pleasant for Mother.

"It's about time you two came in," said Mrs. Devery.

Stella announced her wish at once. "I'd like to visit Robin's house every morning and pose for her," she told her grandmother.

Mrs. Devery moved her ringed hands uneasily. "But how are you going to get there and get home? I don't think it's safe for you to go to a strange house. I don't think—"

"I'll come for her in the morning," Robin offered quickly. "I'll come at ten o'clock and bring her home at twelve."

"Good!" said Mrs. Ward. "Then everything is settled. I'm sure Stella will enjoy this, and Robin will be grateful."

For the moment Mrs. Devery was overwhelmingly defeated, but she did not give in without a counterattack. She fixed her granddaughter with a look of disapproval and spoke critically. "As I've told you before, Stella, I will not have you wearing blue jeans on Sunday. Our visitors will think you have no good clothes to dress in properly."

"I couldn't find anything else," Stella objected. "When you came home from church this morning, you changed everything around in my room so it would suit you. So how can I know where anything is?"

Mrs. Devery looked startled and again at a loss for an answer. Stella seemed pleased with herself and a little smug. For the first time Robin found that she felt almost sorry for Mrs. Devery. Stella was no one to waste tears over. She was at war with her grandmother and she had enjoyed this chance to put her in the wrong.

What an unhappy way that would be to live, Robin thought. Of course there were fights in her own family. There were times when she told herself that she did not like her mother or her father or her brother. Yet all the while she knew this wasn't true. She knew very well that underneath momentary anger and disagreements there was always understanding. And there was love. Between Stella Devery and her grandmother there was no love. Stella's blindness was a fact, and by now Robin could understand that it must be accepted as such and no pity wasted on her because of it. But a life devoid of loving understanding was truly something Robin Ward could feel sorry about.

All this came in one of those swift moments of comprehension Robin sometimes experienced. It took no longer than the time of following her mother toward the door. Before she stepped into the hall, Robin looked up and saw something that brought her to a halt and dashed everything else from her mind.

Near the wall, by the door, was a tier of whatnot

shelves. As Robin glanced at them she saw that a well-polished object of brass sat on the second shelf. It looked like a small incense burner, with a circular base that sat on three stubby legs. The lid to the burner fitted neatly and was topped by a small, decorative temple dog playing with a ball.

Mother was at the front door, waiting, and Robin followed her. This was not the time to ask questions, yet she was sure that the last time she had seen that lid it had been unpolished and grimy with dirt, and it had been left for safekeeping on a ledge beneath the birdbath on the Wards' front lawn.

(8)

The Strangeness of Stella Devery

MONDAY WAS ANOTHER clear, hot day. Robin rose early, in anticipation of Stella's visit. Right after breakfast she went upstairs to see about working arrangements. Last night she had asked Dad to move the round oak table from the library into her room. It would make a good working table, though it did take up a lot of room.

Now it occurred to her that a better arrangement was possible. After Dad had gone to work, Robin asked her mother to come upstairs.

"It's going to be such a hot day. And my balcony is cool and shady in the morning. So couldn't we move the table out there for now?"

Mother looked at the clumsy old thing and shook her head. "It would take a strong man to budge that table, I'm afraid. We'd never manage to get it through the door."

"Isn't Julian coming to cut the grass?" Robin asked. "Maybe the three of us—"

Eventually that was the way it was done. When Julian arrived he was summoned upstairs, and by rocking the table on its big pedestal foot they managed to get it out upon the balcony. Mother went off to fetch modeling equipment. Julian had not been upstairs in their house

103

and he looked around with interest. He seemed pleased to hear that Stella was coming over to pose. But since either Mother or Tommy was around all the time, Robin had no chance to tell Julian that Mr. Lemon was inside the Devery house, though his presence had not been announced by Mrs. Devery. Or that the brass lid had reappeared on top of an incense burner in Mrs. Devery's drawing room.

At the moment, Julian's attention focused on the way the front corner of the Devery house seemed to point directly at the rear corner of the Wards'.

"That's Stella's room where the balcony is on the top floor," Robin told him. "If she could see me, I could wave to her from here."

"You could do better than that," said Julian. "If you want to, you could fix up a message system between your balconies. I've got some nylon line at home and a pulley. I could set it up for you and if you attached a container of some sort to the line, you could send messages back and forth."

"What messages?" Tommy asked. "Why should you send messages when you can holler?"

"That's the scientific mind speaking," Julian laughed. "Never mind, Thomas. I'll bet your sister will work something out."

"When are you going to put it up?" Tommy inquired, interested in the mechanical aspects.

"Not till I talk to Stella about it," Robin said.

Tommy decided to return to what he now claimed was a hydrofoil boat. But before Robin could launch into what she wanted to tell Julian, Mother brought in a big tin container of moist clay, from which the girls could scoop whatever they wished to use. When she had spread a piece of oilcloth over the table, she set out two old chopping boards on which they could work.

When Julian had gone back to his grass-cutting, Mother spoke approvingly of him. "That is a very intelligent boy. He has a good brain and uses it. We're lucky to have the Hornfelds for neighbors. They are going to be good for all of us."

Robin felt a warm glow of pride in Julian, who was already her friend. If only she could make the clay come right so that Mr. Hornfeld would take her into his class, she might learn more of what Julian and he could teach her.

Just before ten o'clock Robin went next door—by way of the lions, and not by the hedge. Stella waited for her on the front steps. This morning she wore a dress of light-blue cotton with patch pockets, and again there was no emerald star pinned to it. Her cap of short brown hair was slightly damp as though she had slicked it down with water. A brooding expression marred her face and she looked far from happy.

Robin called to her so she would know who was approaching. Stella did not brighten, though she stood up and waited for Robin to reach the steps. Mrs. Devery emerged from the house and greeted Robin in her chill, disapproving way. It was clear that she did not like the idea of Stella going next door, but had been unable to find any logical reason for preventing it.

The two girls escaped as quickly as possible, and again Stella walked with her hand in the crook of Robin's arm. She seemed to move with greater uncertainty this morning and even when they left the Devery house behind, she did not cheer up.

Robin was learning the best way to guide the other

girl. She walked a little ahead, and paused for the curb, mentioning it. She would say, "Now to the left," before they turned in that direction, or "Turn right now" when needed, but without chattering constant directions.

Mother was waiting to greet them, and they went upstairs to Robin's room. Stella seemed increasingly listless and lacking in interest. She allowed herself to be led, and took no interest in her new surroundings. Such changes of mood were hard to keep up with, and Robin felt both discouraged and disappointed.

Mother gave each girl a coverall apron and saw them seated at the round oak table on the shady balcony. She opened the can of clay and gave Stella a good-sized lump to work with. She had set out various "tools" for them to use. Mostly these were wooden tongue depressors, such as doctors used, orangewood sticks, some spoons, and a blunt knife. There was also a stick with a wire loop at one end which was a proper clay tool. Then she went away, leaving the girls alone.

Feeling clumsy, though she was no stranger to clay, Robin dug out a large lump for herself. The clay was fresh and moist and slightly slippery to the touch. Being the nonceramic kind, there was no need to worry about preparing it for firing, and she could go right to work. Since she did not want to use an armature on which to form the head, it was necessary to build up a solid mass that would hold together when the planes of the face and the shape of the chin were cut away.

From time to time as she worked she glanced at Stella. There was little that seemed appealing about her this morning. She had a tendency to duck her head and close her eyes, as though by doing so she could hide herself from Robin's gaze. As far as the clay went, she

seemed to be pulling it apart and sticking it together without trying to make anything.

There couldn't be much neck allowed without an armature to hold it up, but building up a block of clay about the size of Stella's head was easy enough for Robin. Now she began to study the general measurements of Stella's head and face. A real sculptor would, of course, use calipers so that he could work exactly to scale, but Robin measured by eye and by pencil held at arm's length as she did when drawing, and quite a bit by guess. She was eager to get past the mechanical phase and start the real task of capturing the way Stella looked, but she knew she could never come to that part unless she was able to distract her from so despondent a mood.

"Is that man with the lemon drops still in the house?" Robin asked.

Stella's expression did not change. She looked surprisingly vindictive and not at all like the girl Robin had wanted to model.

"I asked Grandmother who he was after you left yesterday," Stella said. "She didn't think I knew he was in the house. When she found out that I did, she let him come downstairs and have dinner with us. He has horrid manners. I hate the way he sucks his food."

"But who is he?" Robin persisted. "Didn't your grandmother explain?"

"She told Mother he was a distant relative of her husband's family—the Deverys—and that he might visit us for a few days."

"A relative! So that's why she let him in. Did she say what his name is?"

"She called him Mr. Lemon, but she doesn't tell lies

very well and I knew it was a made-up name when she said it. She says he hasn't been feeling well and he is going to stay quiet and rest for a while. Which sounds as though he might be hiding from something. Grandmother said not to mention his being there to anyone outside." A faint look of mischief showed around Stella's mouth. "I told her you and Julian already knew about him."

"What did she say?" Robin felt slightly aghast.

"Nothing. Later I asked Mother how she looked when I mentioned that and she said Grandmother and Mr. Lemon both got red in the face. Mother said Mr. Lemon seemed angry, and she had the feeling that Grandmother was worried about something. I wish I knew what it is about him that I can't remember."

"What do you mean?" Robin asked.

Stella shook her head and was silent. She had begun to work idly with the lump of clay before her, and Robin saw that she was forming some sort of grotesque object out of it—a thing of lumps and crooked angles that Robin could not identify as anything either animal or human.

She told Stella about her experience in finding the incense burner lid and of how it had disappeared, only to show up again on the burner itself in Mrs. Devery's drawing room. Stella, however, knew nothing of such a burner and did not seem especially interested.

"Have you done my face yet?" she asked, thumping and twisting the clay.

As her discouragement grew, Robin began to feel short-tempered. "Of course not!" So far all she had was the rough shape that she kept building and smoothing, always discovering that it did not in any way resemble the form of Stella's head. "I expect it will take me days and days to get this done." September suddenly seemed too close. Much too close. She turned the cutting board so she could work on the other side. Then she got up and walked around Stella, trying to see her as a whole, trying to get a feeling about the planes of her face. One of the difficulties of working in the round was that the result had to look right from all angles.

"What are you doing?" Stella said. When Robin had explained, she went on. "Grandmother won't let me come here for long. She's looking for a good reason to stop me now. Can't you work any faster than that?"

As she sat down again, Robin decided to be frank. "Today you're different—so how can I hurry? The look that made me want to see if I could catch your face in clay is gone. Is something the matter?"

Stella ducked her head toward the grotesque object that was growing in her fingers. When she spoke again, her tone was defiant. "Grandmother says there are only two reasons why you would invite me over here. One is that you're sorry for me because I'm blind. And the other is that you want to get something from me—like having me pose for you. She says I should have pride enough not to come."

Robin tipped over the egg shape that was somehow all wrong and rolled it indignantly into a long fat worm. Her patience had run out. "I do want something from you! I thought we might be friends and that you'd help me. At first you wanted to. But if you believe such unpleasant things, I might as well take you home right now."

For a moment Stella looked astonished. She held up the strange, distorted thing she had formed in the clay.

"This is my grandmother," she announced and pounded the ugly shape flat with both fists—as a child in kindergarten might have done.

Robin felt suddenly frightened. There was something hateful in the movement of Stella's hands, something almost cruel in the way she destroyed the ugly thing she had made. In an instant she had turned from a girl of twelve to a child of five or six who was having a tantrum and breaking up her toys.

The change was so alarming that Robin wondered whether she should call her mother. This modeling session that she had looked forward to sharing with Stella had turned out all wrong.

Quietly Robin pushed her chair back from the table, but at once Stella was alert. She reached out and put a hand on Robin's arm.

"Where are you going?" she demanded.

Robin had the eerie feeling that Stella's fingers might tighten until they hurt and that Stella might try to treat her as she had the clay.

"Perhaps you don't like working in clay?" Robin asked, trying to hide her uneasiness. "I—I thought I'd ask my mother if—" but she did not know what excuse to offer. If *what?*

Stella withdrew her hand. "Don't go. Of course I like working in clay. I think I'll try to make Herr Binglebaum."

She located the edge of the board she was working on, and then the farther edge of the table, as she did occasionally, and picked up an orangewood stick. Without warning the storm was over.

Robin could only sit back in her chair and watch helplessly. She had not the faintest notion how to get her own clay piece started. In fact, she no longer had the feeling that she wanted to make anything of it. It was hard to concentrate while Stella was here, and Robin gave up any pretense of working.

(9)

Whisper of Guns

As ROBIN SAT with bits of clay drying on her fingers, she watched a shape that was quite a bit like Herr Bingle-baum taking form beneath Stella's hands. But she could not forget the ugly, monstrous thing Stella had made and called her grandmother.

"Do you know that your grandmother was very beautiful as a girl?" Robin asked. "There's a portrait of her hanging over the mantel in your drawing room. She looked a lot like you when she was eighteen."

Stella's hands were still. "What *is* beautiful? Can you tell me what beautiful is?"

It came to Robin that beauty of a visual sort was something as far beyond Stella's knowledge as a conception of the sky, or comprehension of the stars, or of colors.

"Can't you tell how your grandmother looks through your fingers?" Robin asked.

"I don't need to touch her," Stella said. "I can hear her, can't I? Besides, I don't go around feeling people's faces." She smiled in amusement. "When I was little I wanted to do that, but my father made me understand that people might not like it. So now I don't touch unless it's someone special. Anyway, I can tell more by a voice

113

and the way a person moves around and sounds to me. And I can tell a lot about hands. They're easier to touch and they tell me about age and a person's size. I can remember how gentle my Cuban grandmother's hands were."

The thought seemed to remind her of something. She wiped her fingers on a cloth Mother had provided and reached into a pocket. Even before she drew them out, Robin knew with a sinking feeling what her fingers would hold. Stella had brought the emerald star after all. Calmly she pinned it to the collar of her dress.

"Thank you for keeping this for me the other day. Grandmother has absolutely forbidden me to wear it. She would be furious if she knew I brought it today. But since she doesn't have any right to stop me, I don't pay any attention. I wear it when she's not around."

"But if it's valuable and you should lose it—" Robin began.

"It belongs to me!" Stella covered the five points of the star with her fingers. "My *abuela,* my Cuban grandmother, gave it to me when she was ill and knew she was going to die. Her family was wealthy long ago and she had some pieces of fine jewelry. After the revolution most of them had to be sold, but this was a pin I always loved when I was small and she said it was to be mine. She said that since I couldn't see the stars in the sky, I could hold one of them in my hand. She was the person who wanted me to be named for a star—Stella. When they found out I would never be able to see, she still wanted the name for me. When I was old enough to understand, she told me I must hold to my star and never let not seeing it defeat me. She was such a—a wonderful person." There was a break in Stella's voice as she went on. "She was nothing like my American grandmother, who thinks that because I'm blind I can't do anything."

Robin found that she was blinking hard to keep back the tears. Nevertheless, she felt sorry for Mrs. Devery, who had been made into an ugly clay thing and smashed to bits.

"Perhaps your grandmother is worried about you," she suggested.

"Then she ought to stop," said Stella. Her fingers touched the star again. "This tells me what I can be if I try hard enough. My mother has explained it to her, but all Grandmother thinks about is how I will hurt myself if I'm left alone, and how there are valuable stones in this pin and it mustn't be worn until I grow up. *Abuela* didn't mean for me to wait. She knew I needed it now."

"Is any of your family left in Cuba?"

"No. There was no one except my mother and me. My father wanted us to get away to safety, and his mother, here on Staten Island, said she would take us if we could come."

Stella went back to work on the comical dog she was making. The figure was quite good, Robin saw—not exactly like Balmy, but with a long, exaggerated body and huge ears that hung down, almost getting in the way of stubby forelegs. As she watched it take shape in Stella's clever fingers, Robin was glad she had decided not to model a dog. She noted how neatly and carefully Stella worked. Now and then she touched the rim of the table to locate it so that she would not knock anything off. And when she put down one of her tools, she remembered where it was so she could find it again without fumbling. Robin, having picked up the blunt knife idly, put it back where Stella had left it. She was learning fast the things she must do to help her visitor.

As for her own work, nothing had come of it. She tried once more to build up the mass that would represent a head, and she began to slice away the clay in order to shape the necessary planes for cheeks and forehead, but the wonder of her dream had vanished as surely as though it had never been. Although Stella was looking more cheerful, the inspiration was gone. The clay seemed to resist her and there was no cleverness in her fingers. Was this going to be worse than the piano-playing? Must she give up before she had even begun? Of course portraiture was hard—she knew that. Nevertheless, she hated to accept so quick a defeat.

A breeze had risen at last, stirring through the hot morning. Stella raised her head, listening to the rustle of leaves, breathing the air deeply.

"Sometimes on Staten Island I feel as if I were in Cuba," she said. "Sometimes I can smell the sea. Now I can smell pine trees too. There are woods behind our houses, aren't there? I'd love to go for a walk."

"I'll take you any time you like," Robin offered. "You can let me know when you're ready." She remembered the suggestion Julian had made about a message system and told Stella about his idea. For a moment the other girl looked interested, but when Robin finished, she shook her head.

"I couldn't read any messages you'd write me, and it wouldn't be any fun to take them to someone else to be read. I can only read and write in Braille, you know. You couldn't read a message from me, either."

Robin had not thought of that. She sighed in disappointment. "I keep forgetting that you're blind."

Stella's bright smile rewarded her. "That's the nicest thing you've said to me. I'm glad you don't keep thinking about it. Not that other people don't forget too, but they forget in the wrong way. My grandmother thinks about it all the time and hates my being blind. She feels that if my father hadn't gone to Cuba and married my mother, she might have had a granddaughter with sight. She'll never forgive any of us for that. But when she walks me around the house, or outdoors, she holds my arm and pushes me. She never sees steps or corners coming up until she runs me into them."

This was more of the sort of thing Robin hated to hear. She spoke on sudden inspiration. "Stella—could I learn Braille?"

While she worked on the dog figure, Stella had stopped ducking her head as though she wanted to hide. Now she turned her face in Robin's direction and her eyes that were so lovely and natural seemed to meet Robin's gaze.

"Of course you could," she said eagerly. "It would be easier for you than for me because I have to do it by touch. If you studied the Braille alphabet, you could read it by sight. And of course you could write it too— though you'd have to do that in reverse, you know."

Robin knew nothing about it, but she listened with interest while Stella explained the Braille cell to her— that remarkable combination of six dots $\vdots$ from which any word could be written. Stella explained what a Braille slate was like too, with its metal form that slid over a piece of paper and enabled one to press dots into the paper with a stylus. Because the dots had to be read from the other side of the paper, it was necessary to reverse them as you pressed them into the paper. Writing had to be done from right to left so it could be read the normal way when turned over.

Down in the backyard Balmy began to bark an excited greeting, and Robin looked over the rail to see Julian putting the lawn mower away.

"Can you come up for a minute?" she called. "We'd like to ask you about the idea you had for a message system."

Julian said, "I'll go home to get some things and come right back."

While they waited, Stella put the finishing touches on the clay dog. Robin had no further wish to touch her own lumpy effort. Her helplessness to make anything out of it brought a discouraging feeling of defeat.

When Julian came upstairs he carried a length of nylon cord, a couple of small pulleys, and two tiny bells that tinkled as he walked.

"I took them off our cat's collar," he said. "If we put a bell at this end of the line and one at Stella's end, you'll be able to signal each other when you've sent a message."

Robin found a small basket, once used for Easter eggs, and Julian said it would be fine to hang on the line. He worked quickly and before long everything was ready on Robin's balcony. Then he dropped the ball of nylon cord to the ground, with its pulley attached. Later he would toss it up to the balcony outside Stella's room, he said. In the meantime, Stella was to keep the bell and fasten it onto her end of the line when she was ready to use it. Without mentioning the fact, they all seemed agreed not to consult Mrs. Devery about their plan.

The bell clinked cheerfully—a small, secret sound— as Stella thrust it into the pocket of her dress. She unpinned the emerald star and put that away along with the bell.

"It's time for me to go home," she said, touching the Braille watch on her left wrist. The lid snapped open so that she could feel the hands lightly and find the dots that told her what time it was. "What shall I do with my clay?" she asked Robin.

For the first time Julian looked at what the girls had been making. When he saw Stella's dog, he exclaimed in approval.

"This is awfully good!" he said. "I'd like to show it to Dad. Would you mind if I borrowed it, Stella?"

A look of happiness had lighted Stella's face at his praise and Robin watched her a little sadly. She was glad for Stella's pleasure, truly glad that her effort in clay had turned out so well. But the bright look on her face reminded Robin of her own foolish dream that she might bring that look to life in clay. She reached for her own hopeless effort, intending to put it back into the container so the clay could be used again.

Julian's observant gaze missed nothing. "Things didn't work out right for you today—is that it?" he said.

"Maybe Mother was right and I'm trying something that's out of my reach," Robin said gloomily.

"You haven't really tried yet, have you?" Julian tapped the lump of clay. "It's still in there, you know."

Robin looked at the lifeless wad she was packing into the tin. "What do you mean?"

"There's an old story Dad likes to tell his students. It's about a child who was watching a great sculptor work in marble. The child came back every day and watched until one day he saw what was coming to light in the marble. He looked at the sculptor in wonder and said, 'How did you know there was a lion in there?' "

The story spoke to her unexpectedly. Robin put the lid tightly on the can while a wonder like that of the child grew in her mind. She knew that Stella's face was there in the clay. It could be brought out so others could see it only if she kept working, kept trying. She could imagine nothing more wonderful than to have the clay reveal the dream that glimmered again in her mind.

"I'll try tomorrow," she told Julian, and he seemed to accept without surprise her willingness to return to her effort. He, at least, did not expect her to give up.

He picked up the wooden board with Stella's wet clay piece on it, and the three went downstairs. Stella held the board for Julian, and Robin watched as he caught up the ball of cord, walking toward the Devery hedge with it in his hands. With a strong throw he hurled it accurately high into the air toward the upper balcony. The cord spun out, shining like silver in the sun, cleared the top of the hedge and disappeared to fall with a thud as the metal pulley struck the balcony floor.

"I heard it land!" Stella cried. "I'll pull it tight and fasten it when I go up to my room."

She gave the clay model back to Julian, and Robin walked next door with her, through the lion gate and toward the house. As they reached the front steps, Stella tensed, listening. Voices reached them from the drawing room, where long glass doors stood open on the veranda. The voices of a man and a woman.

Stella pulled Robin off the walk and down behind the snowball bush that grew below the veranda's edge. White petals sprinkled them as they knelt, clinging to Stella's brown hair.

"Can they see us from here?" she whispered.

Startled, Robin peered over the bushes. The doors were safely distant across the veranda, so no one could glimpse them crouching here.

"I don't think so," she said uncomfortably.

Stella nodded in satisfaction. "Ever since he came, Mr. Lemon has been having long talks with my grandmother. She closes the doors to shut Mother and me out, and talks to him for hours. I wish I knew what it was all about."

Now and then words reached them clearly as they knelt behind the bushes, but in spite of the fact that she was curious, Robin hated to listen. She knew this was something Stella shouldn't be doing, and that it might get them both into trouble. But before she could draw Stella away, Mr. Lemon said something in a hoarse whisper that came to them clearly and Robin felt her skin turn cold in terror.

"The guns are to be found," he said. "I know where to get them."

"Hush!" said Mrs. Devery.

Robin, holding her breath, heard someone cross to the glass doors and close them. After that she could hear only a murmur of voices.

"Guns!" Stella whispered. "Why is he telling my grandmother about guns? Oh, I wish I could think why his voice reminds me of something! I'm sure it's something unpleasant, but I don't know what."

Stella had said the same sort of thing before, Robin recalled, but she did not want to ask questions now.

"Let's not stay here," Robin pleaded. "It would be awful if they found us hiding and listening."

Stella agreed only because they could hear nothing more. "Thanks for bringing me home. After a time or two I can come by myself. I'll go upstairs and see if I can get the other end of that line fastened on my balcony."

"I'll call for you at the same time tomorrow," Robin said. "You will come, won't you?"

"I hope so," said Stella and went up the steps and into the house.

Robin threw rules aside and escaped from the Devery grounds by crawling hurriedly through the hole in the hedge. She wanted to get away as quickly as possible. A house in which a man seemed to be hiding—a man who whispered secretly of guns—was not a place near which she wanted to linger. Something was terribly wrong and it was hard to imagine why a woman like Stella's grandmother would be mixed up in such goings-on.

She wished she had asked Stella to find out whatever she could about that incense burner. There was still the queer matter to be solved of who could have taken the lid from beneath the birdbath and restored it to the object Mrs. Devery had found in the rubble of that house across the street.

When Robin went upstairs to her room, she found her mother looking around the balcony. "You'll clean everything up, won't you, Robin?" she asked.

Robin nodded. "When I'm through. I might try again this afternoon by myself."

"How did it go this morning?" Mother asked.

Robin told her of the amusing figure of a dog Stella had made and of how Julian had taken it to show his father. But when it came to her own work, she could only shake her head.

"I still think you're trying something much too hard," her mother said.

Robin put a hand on the tin of clay. "I do know how hard it is. But it's all in here. I can't give up without trying to get it out."

Mother went off looking doubtful, and Robin left the balcony and went into her room. It was nearly lunchtime and she didn't want to get the clay out again now. But at least the urge to try another time was strongly alive in her. She wanted to prove her mother wrong. She wanted to show Julian what she could do. She wanted to have something to submit for Mr. Hornfeld's judgment and enter his class. But most of all, she wanted to do this thing successfully herself, with her own hands. She wanted to make her dream real and find the lion in the clay.

A writer must feel like this about writing a book, she thought. And an artist about painting a picture. Perhaps it was the same with everyone who wanted to create something. The scientist engaged in research must feel this way. First there was a dream—the image of what might be possible. And then you had to find the way to make the dream a reality. If you gave up, if you didn't try, you had nothing.

The faint tinkle of a bell caught her attention and she ran out onto the balcony. Stella's balcony was empty and there was no one at her window, but the straw basket must have been pulled across the line and sent back. There was something in it, weighted down.

Robin lifted out the weight and found that it was a smooth, bluish-gray stone, polished to a gloss, so that it was pleasantly smooth to the touch. Under it lay two filing cards. As she took them from the basket she saw that one had been punched with three rows of dots. She sat at the table with a pencil in hand and wrote the letters of the alphabet above each group of dots. It came out exactly right and she knew that Stella had sent her a complete Braille alphabet.

A	B	C	D	E	F	G	H	I

J	K	L	M	N	O	P	Q	R

S	T	U	V	W	X	Y	Z

The second card bore a few of the punched-in dots. Using the code of the alphabet, she took only a little while to locate the various groups of dots and identify the words. She finished with a sense of triumph and read the message: "Thank you." The dots below were easy to identify because she could guess that they spelled "Stella." She wished that she could send an answer, but since that did not seem possible without any equipment, she looked through a drawer in her room and found a sample bottle of perfume to put with the polished stone. She sent the basket on its return journey, pulling at the cord that would ring the bell. Nothing happened on the other balcony, so Stella was probably elsewhere. She would find the small gift later. Now it was lunchtime, and Robin hurried to wash and run downstairs.

For the rest of that day she saw nothing of Stella, nothing of anyone next door. Her mother kept her busy with chores around the house, since the Wards were still

getting settled. Once when she had time, she ran upstairs to her room and checked the contents of the basket.
The perfume flask was gone, but this time there was no
message.

Not until evening was the Devery house heard from
once more. The Wards were sitting on the veranda in
the cool of dusk, listening to Dad talk about his experiences during his first day at the museum, when Balmy
jumped from his place beside Robin and began to bark.

A voice called to them from the walk. "Please—I may
speak with you?"

The voice was that of Stella's mother, and Robin's
heart began to settle in the direction of her shoes. This,
she knew instinctively, was going to be bad news.

(10)

Encounter in the Woods

DAD BROUGHT a chair for Mrs. Devery and coaxed her to sit down. Mother went inside for another cool glass of her special mixture. A soft light fell upon the porch from a lamp in the living room and Robin could see the anxious, hesitant look on the face of Stella's mother. As she sipped her drink, she looked as though she wanted to jump up and rush right back home.

Mother talked about the pleasant evening to put her at ease and mentioned that Stella had seemed to enjoy being here this morning. That brought the younger Mrs. Devery to the point of her visit.

"I am very sorry," she said in her soft voice with its Spanish inflection. "This is why I come. Stella's grandmother does not wish her to return tomorrow."

Robin made a sound of disappointment and the pretty Cuban woman went on quickly. "Her grandmother believes Stella becomes too much excited today. She feels this is not good for her and she does not wish her to continue."

"What do you wish?" Mother asked.

Mrs. Devery looked startled at being consulted. "What can I say? We must stay with my husband's mother. We have nowhere to go. My husband wished

126

us to come here. We must do as he wished, as his mother wishes."

"Do you think your daughter was made overly excited by her visit today?" Dad asked gently.

For a moment the Cuban woman stared into her glass, tinkling the ice against its sides, as if she might seek an answer there. When she looked up her expression had changed. She was no longer meek and submissive, but rebellious.

"For me, I think it is better if Stella has something to excite her. She lives too much alone. She misses her friends in Havana—though of course much is changed there now. I am pleased that she comes to see your daughter. But my husband's mother does not listen when I try to explain. She believes her own way is always right."

"Then we'll have to do something to change her mind," Mother said resolutely.

Mrs. Devery put her unfinished glass aside and stood up hastily. "Please—it is better not to oppose my mother-in-law. I am grateful to you and to Robin. But for now, it is better—" Her voice trailed off. The momentary spark was gone, and one sensed that this woman who had suffered so much grief and discouragement was trying to find her way in a strange place. It was understandable that she wanted to cause no trouble. She said good night and left them quickly, as though she did not dare to express herself further.

Mother watched her disappear toward the street and clicked her tongue disapprovingly. "Agnes Devery is a tyrant! We've got to stop this. She can't be allowed to treat that child as if she were a prisoner."

"Whoa!" Dad said. "Easy does it. Better not do anything hasty. You might make everything that much worse."

From a dark corner where he had been nearly forgotten, Tommy spoke up suddenly. "I'll bet it's that Mr. Lemon making trouble. He doesn't want any visitors over there. And he doesn't want Stella to go around talking about him."

Robin threw her brother an astonished glance.

Dad said, "Who is Mr. Lemon?" and Tommy told him he was a man staying at the Deverys'.

Mother said reluctantly, "All right—I'll be careful. But I'm not going to give up. It's the best possible thing for that child to get out and meet someone her own age."

"I agree," Dad said. "And it's just as important for Robin to know her."

Robin nodded vigorous agreement. Dad understood how much she could learn from Stella. No one was merely being kind, as old Mrs. Devery thought. Stella was *someone*—a person, as Julian had pointed out—and worth knowing for herself. Robin hoped Mother would be cautious. Sometimes her approach was sweepingly direct in the way a storm was direct—and could cause as much damage.

Robin slipped away from the others and went upstairs. The container of clay still waited for her on the balcony. Through the trees Stella's room showed no light, so she must not be there. If only there was an easy way to reach her, talk to her. Robin recalled that Stella had been there alone in her dark room the time when her mother had come in. Of course! There was no need for a girl who could not see to turn on a light. How strange that seemed. There was so much about blindness that a sighted person had to think about and try to understand. It was possible that Stella was in her room, but Robin dared not call to her. That would bring Mrs. Devery upstairs to see what was going on, and perhaps to forbid even that. But there might be another way to communicate.

Robin ran down the hall to the library and rummaged in her father's desk until she found a filing card like the ones Stella had used for her Braille message. Then she returned to her own room and tried ways of pressing dots into the card. A pin was too sharp, but the point of a blunt pencil forced a raised dot on the opposite side of the card. Perhaps there was a way in which she could send a message to Stella after all. A lovely idea had occurred to her—something Mrs. Devery had not yet forbidden.

Earnestly Robin went to work, studying the alphabet Stella had sent her, pressing the right set of dots into the card to form two words that would not make too long a message. Luckily, she remembered that the dots she pressed into the paper must be read from the opposite side. This made it harder, but Robin managed to set the letters down properly by copying them backward in pencil first. When she was through, she turned the card over and felt the dots with her fingers. They weren't as neat as they should be, and perhaps her spacing wasn't accurate since she had no Braille slate to guide her. But perhaps Stella would be able to read the words: WOODS TOMORROW.

The basket waited at her side of the balcony. Robin slipped the card under the stone weight, sent it back across space, and rang Stella's bell. She could not see the other girl in the darkness, but she heard her come out on the balcony, find the basket, and take the card out of it. Stella went inside and there was silence for a while. Robin waited anxiously. If only Stella could understand what she had written.

Before long, she heard sounds from the opposite balcony. The bell at Robin's end tinkled and the basket came swiftly back to her. The card Robin had sent was in the basket. When she took it inside, she saw that a new row of dots had been added below her own. She went to work at once and soon deciphered the new message. It, too, was short, and much neater than Robin's dots had been. This time there were four words: BACK GATE AT TEN.

Wonderful! Robin had a date with Stella. Tomorrow morning nothing would keep her from the back gate of the Devery property, and she would take Stella for a walk in the woods.

In her excitement and high elation over the success of her effort, she took a pencil and piece of paper and sat down in her room. She had always liked to sketch and she knew that sculptors made drawings of various features of their models to help in their work. Now she did several sketches of Stella's mouth, trying the lines this way and that. What she achieved wasn't perfect, but it was far closer than anything she had managed in the clay. She was beginning to find her way.

When she went to bed that night, the assignment she had given herself no longer seemed so foolish and hopeless as when Stella was here this morning. Her fingers had to practice first. They had to be comfortable in the clay. She wasn't going to give up this time. She was going to see this through.

The next morning she hurried with her chores, setting her room thoroughly to rights before she went in search of her mother. This time she was hanging curtains in the living room. She seemed to spend most of her life on stepladders these days.

"Do you care if I go for a walk in the woods?" Robin asked.

Mother formed a pinch pleat so that it suited her exactly before she gave Robin a long, thoughtful look. "All that bell tinkling last night," she said. "I knew something was up. You're going for a walk with Stella?"

Robin smiled at her sheepishly. "You don't care, do you? Nobody told us not to."

"That might be splitting hairs," Mother said. "But in this case I'm for splitting them. Good for you! I'm working on a new idea and I'll let you know how it develops."

"You won't make Mrs. Devery mad?" Robin asked anxiously.

"Not any madder than you'll make her when she finds you've taken Stella for a walk."

They looked at each other with a secret smile, like two conspirators, and Robin was glad her father wasn't there to caution them.

Ten o'clock seemed a long time in coming. Surreptitiously Robin kept an eye on the Devery house and saw a tall, thin woman with a bun of gray hair at the back of her head carrying out garbage pails for the morning pickup truck. Flora was apparently working today. Mr. Lemon did not appear—whether Robin looked through the hole in the hedge, or down from her high balcony. Stella's mother, of course, had gone off to work.

At ten minutes before ten, Robin saw Mrs. Devery come out of the house carrying a pile of library books. These she placed in the front seat of her car, and backed it from the garage. Then she drove out of the court. That was a real break. If she was going to pick out new books at the library, Stella could be free for a while. Though Robin did not know whether Flora might interfere.

As soon as Mrs. Devery had gone, Robin took Balmy's leash and fastened it to his collar. Herr Binglebaum would love a walk in the woods. Tommy, fortunately, was not around to ask questions. Robin lifted Balmy to the top of the stone wall that ran behind the Ward property and climbed up beside him. Together girl and dog dropped to the soft carpet of pine needles and dry leaves that edged the woods beyond the wall.

Balmy was beside himself with joy. He wanted to dash off in all directions at once, but Robin held firmly to his leash and followed the wall to the place where it met the higher wall behind Devery property. This wall was higher and would be hard to climb. Fortunately, there was a gate. Robin could look through it into the Devery backyard.

She had not long to wait before Stella came out on the back porch, talking to Flora. Like Robin, she wore jeans today and again the emerald star was pinned to her blouse. When she opened the gate, Robin waved to Flora.

She was about to say, "I'll look after her," but managed to stop herself. Who wanted to be looked after all the time? Instead, she called, "We'll be fine. I'm taking my dog along."

Flora waved back sympathetically and went inside.

"Hello," Stella said, sounding pleased and a little shy.

Robin gave her arm a happy squeeze and let her pat Balmy before they set off down the path that wound beneath trees. The wooded area occupied some four blocks that stretched between Catalpa Court and streets lower down the hill. No one had built here, and the trees and brush had grown unchecked for many years, offering a miniature forest that neighborhood children enjoyed.

Again Stella walked a little behind, with her hand in the crook of Robin's arm, sensing her every movement. She managed well, in spite of the curving dirt path, placing her feet naturally as she walked and trusting Robin not to run her into a tree. She did so well that Robin had to say so and Stella seemed pleased.

"My father taught me how to walk in the very beginning," she said. "He wouldn't let me drag my feet the way some blind people do. He wouldn't let me step too high either, and he made me hold up my head. He walked me over all sorts of ground and into strange places so that I would put my feet down like other people."

"Could you get a trained dog to help you?" Robin asked.

"Not until I'm older. If I want one then. Not everyone can do well with a dog. And dogs take a lot of looking after. Some blind people would rather use a cane."

Balmy was being no help on this walk, and Robin wished she could let him off on his own. He ran around them and got his leash into a snarl, and he always wanted to go in an opposite direction from the one Robin chose. Balmy needed training in walking himself, she decided.

"What about Mr. Lemon?" she asked as they neared a place where the path came into the open on a steep hillside and a wide view stretched out below them.

Stella looked worried. "I know there's something wrong. I think he's trying to make Grandmother do something she doesn't want to do. I know she's upset. I can hear it in her voice and in the sound of her steps when she walks around the house. She didn't sound this way before he came."

Stella paused on the path and pulled back from the steep pitch of the hillside. "We've come out of the woods, haven't we? I can feel the change in the air. The sounds are different. Even the smell of the air is different."

Robin glanced at her in surprise. It was certainly foolish to think blind people were helpless, as Mrs. Devery believed.

"We're on the rim of a steep hillside," Robin said. "We can see out over the rooftops below, clear across the Kill van Kull to New Jersey."

The Kill had been named by the Dutch settlers of Staten Island and it was the channel that circled this part of the island, dividing it from New Jersey.

"Tell me what you see," Stella urged.

Robin tried. "There's an industrial section on the nearest land over in New Jersey, and there are dozens of big round tanks clustered there. They've been painted pink and blue and green and yellow—so they are almost pretty to look at."

Then she remembered that colors meant nothing to Stella, that perhaps she didn't know what was meant by a tank.

The other girl seemed to understand her troubled silence. "I know the names of colors," she assured Robin. "Dad said I had to learn about colors so I could dress myself properly and not wear things that clash because colors are important to other people. Robin— am I dressed right now? I put my things away in special places so I can find them. With some of my clothes I sew on markers where they won't show, to tell me what color a dress or a blouse is. When I feel a snap under a collar seam it means blue to me, for instance. Grandmother doesn't understand this and she mixed everything up. I'm getting my clothes back in place, but I'm not sure of everything yet."

"You look fine," Robin said, marveling that Stella could sew. "Blue jeans and a blue shirt go nicely together. And the red ribbon around your hair looks nice too."

"Thank you," Stella said.

"How does where we are now seem to you?" Robin asked.

The other girl explained readily. "I can feel the wind, of course, and smell the pine trees, and other green things growing. I heard a squirrel back there in the woods. He was chattering and scampering along a branch right over our heads. And there were birds twittering. I can feel the sun on my face and my arms when we walk out of the shade of the trees. I can hear branches rustling and creaking when the wind blows. Under my feet the leaves and pine needles feel soft and springy, like a carpet, and when I brush against a tree I like the rough feeling of the bark. Way off somewhere I can hear children shouting. And sometimes there's a whistle from a boat down there on the Kill. There's more too—so much more."

"You're not blind," said Robin softly. "I think you see more than I do in a lot of ways."

Stella spoke fiercely. "I have to work at it. I don't dare get lazy. Dad used to say it would be easy to sit still and feel sorry for myself because I can't see what other people see. But he would never let me do that. Even when I was little he used to put things into my hands and make me tell him all I could about them."

Together they went on as the path curved back into the woods. Once more Balmy tried to make off into the brush to chase a robin that could never be caught.

"I found that incense burner that you told me about," Stella said as they walked along. "I took it down from the shelf in the drawing room and had a look at it."

Robin was no longer surprised when Stella used words like "see" and "look." She realized that there was more than one way of seeing and that much of Stella's sight was in her fingertips.

"The lid you told me about feels as though it fits—as if it had been made for the rest of the burner. And you were right about the doglike thing on top, with a ball between its paws. It's made of brass. I can tell brass because it squeaks if I rub it, and it gives my fingers an odd sort of smell."

"Then someone took the lid from the place where I put it and gave it to Mrs. Devery," Robin said. "I don't think she knew where it was herself."

"It was Mr. Lemon," Stella said. "I'm sure of that, because while I had the brass burner in my hands he came into the room and asked me what I was doing with it. I told him that Grandmother said she had found it over in the wreckage of the house across the street, but that it didn't have a lid on it. He said of course it didn't. He was the one who had given her the lid."

"But how queer!" Robin said. "Did he tell you where he found it?"

"No, he didn't say any more about it. He took it away from me and put it back on the shelf, as though it were something I might break—which is silly. But let's not talk about him. Let's walk in the woods again."

The path turned back from the open place on the hill, winding through that part of the woods that led around the Devery property to its far side. They might have been in a deep forest as they went on, for all the houses were shut away from view by dark, crowding trees. The sense of a lonely, deserted place began to deepen, though Robin knew there were people within shouting distance. A big cloud had rolled across the face of the sun. While the rest of the sky was blue and no rain threatened, darkness increased beneath the trees and Robin hesitated on the path. At once Stella stopped, sensing that something was wrong.

"What is it?" she asked. "What's the matter?"

"Let's go back," Robin said. "The trees are getting thicker and it's very dark. I don't like it much."

"Is it like a jungle?" Stella asked. "I've read about jungles. Don't worry—if it gets too dark, I can lead you. Here, let me go ahead."

Before Robin could object, the other girl stepped out along the path. She seemed able to sense the feeling of it beneath her feet, and she moved her hands out lightly to the side, or in front of her, so that the back of a hand would swing into contact with anything that stood in the way. Sometimes she lifted an elbow slightly and accomplished the same thing. Whenever her hand grazed a tree, she turned back to the open path again. She walked slowly and carefully, with Robin following anxiously at her heels and holding onto Balmy's leash.

"You might run into a tree or something," Robin warned uneasily.

"So what?" said Stella. "I run into things all the time, but I do it lightly and it doesn't hurt. Except now and then when I get mixed up."

She was growing a little cocky and pleased with herself—perhaps showing off, so that she became careless. A root growing in a loop across the path betrayed her. Before Robin noticed it was there, Stella caught her toe in it unexpectedly and went down on her knees on the ground.

At once Robin ran to her. "Are you hurt? I didn't see that root. I'm sorry!"

Stella was laughing. "I didn't see it either. Of course I'm not hurt. I'll bet you fall harder than this lots of times. I'm not made of glass, you know."

She did not get up from the ground at once, but sat cross-legged while Balmy leaped upon her with enthusiasm. She held the dog to her while he licked her cheek.

"How warm his coat is, and how smooth," she said. "Is it red like fire, or yellow like sunshine?"

"It's brown," Robin told her. "Brown like—like—"

Stella reached for something that pressed into her leg and held it up. "Brown like a pine cone?" She sniffed at the cone and examined its layers with eager, sensitive fingers. "I love pine cones. They're wonderful, with all those little scallops. But they're brittle and dry—you have to be careful or you break them easily."

Again Robin found herself studying the bright look of Stella's face. She was happy this morning and eagerly alive—as she did not seem to be within her grandmother's shadow.

"Give me your hand," Stella said.

Robin bent toward her and Stella's reaching fingers found one red braid as it fell forward. At once her fingers closed about it gently, sensing its thickness, following its length.

"I didn't know you had a braid," Stella said.

"I've two of them," said Robin. She took Stella's

hands and let them follow the braids right to her head. The other girl's fingers did not stop there. After a brief hesitation they traveled lightly across Robin's face, seeking the shape of her cheeks, following the bridge of her nose and the lift of her lips. Robin kept very still, hardly breathing. Stella had said she did this only with someone special.

"You're awfully nice," the other girl said, laughing. She jumped up and brushed leaves and earth from her jeans. Now she was willing to reach for Robin's arm and they walked together around a bend in the path as it turned toward the Devery house from the far side. Robin, leading the way around the turn, stood suddenly still in dismay, staring at the man who sat upon a fallen tree trunk. A piece of candy plumped out one cheek. He sucked on it noisily, as he regarded them without surprise. Mr. Lemon was waiting for them.

(11)

Tommy Makes a Guess

STELLA HEARD the sucking sound. "It's Mr. Lemon, isn't it?" she said.

"It is, indeed," the fat man informed her quickly. "I've been waiting for you two. I'm glad you came around this way. Otherwise I'd have had to go after you. I found out from Flora where you'd gone and I'm sure you don't have your grandmother's permission to be here, Stella."

A clump of Queen Anne's lace grew beside the path, and he plucked a blossom from a tall stalk, shredding it idly in pudgy fingers. Robin loved Queen Anne's lace. Mother said it was too pretty to be considered a weed and sometimes she brought an armload of it indoors and put it around in vases. Mr. Lemon's act was senselessly destructive.

"Let's go back the way we came," she whispered to Stella.

Mr. Lemon stood up. "Never mind your whispering. I'll take this poor little blind girl home myself. She shouldn't be out playing with someone who can't look after her. She might have hurt herself badly just now. I saw her fall on the path. Were you injured, Stella?"

The bright look had gone out of Stella's face, but she

stood her ground, facing Mr. Lemon, her lower lip stuck out rebelliously. "I'm not a poor little blind girl! And if I want to walk in the woods with Robin, I will. I'm not ready to go home."

"Hoity-toity!" Mr. Lemon said mockingly. "Walking in the woods with an emerald pin on your blouse! I suppose your grandmother is going to be pleased about that?"

"It has a safety catch on it," said Stella. "And I'm not going home."

"Oh, yes you are, young lady. When Cousin Agnes and your mother aren't home, I'm responsible, being your nearest relative."

He came toward the two girls and Robin tried to step in front of her friend, but he pushed past her rudely and took Stella by one elbow. At that moment something completely astonishing happened. Balmy, who loved everybody, must have decided from past acquaintance that he did not, after all, love Mr. Lemon. Without warning, he jerked his leash from Robin's hand and flew for the offender's ankles, nipping and snarling and yapping.

Mr. Lemon let go of Stella and sprang back in alarm. "Get away from me! Call off your dog! Get away, you nasty little beast."

Stella began to laugh as she realized what was happening. "Good for Herr Binglebaum!" she cried. "Sic 'em, Balmy, sic 'em!"

Robin tried in a choked voice to call Balmy back, but she was laughing too. He was too small to do any harm and he wasn't biting, but only yapping at Mr. Lemon's ankles in defense of those to whom his loyalty was given.

Mr. Lemon kicked at Balmy with one foot and when

the dog fell back for a moment, he bent to pick up a heavy branch from the ground. Abruptly what was happening no longer seemed funny. In his hand the branch would make a dangerous club and it was quite clear that he meant to bring it down upon Balmy.

Robin made a dive for the dog and caught him up in her arms. Then she faced the angry little man.

"If you hit him with that stick, I—I'll call the police. And I'll tell them you're hiding in Mrs. Devery's house. I'll tell them about those guns you know about!"

Mr. Lemon lowered the stick. He still looked angry, but now he was pale as well. "Don't get into something you don't understand!" he snapped. "I knew you be-

longed to a meddling family the minute I laid eyes on you. Keep out of my business if you know what's good for you. As for you, Stella, Cousin Agnes is going to hear about what has happened. Especially about your wearing that valuable pin when she has told you not to. Perhaps you had better give it to me for safekeeping."

"I won't!" Stella cried. "I won't!"

Balmy growled and tried to leap out of Robin's arms, and she had to squeeze hard to hold him. Mr. Lemon decided that he did not want to remain within range of the furious little dog, and went off along the path, puffing in his haste. Once he looked behind to see if Balmy was following him.

"He's gone, hasn't he?" Stella said, listening to the hasty retreat. With one hand she had covered the pin on her blouse protectively.

"Yes—he's gone," Robin said. "No—wait—I think he's coming back. I can hear—"

Stella shook her head. "That's someone else. Someone coming from lower down the hill."

Robin whirled to see Julian Hornfeld climbing toward them through the woods, not bothering to follow a path.

"I'm sorry I couldn't get here sooner," he said, out of breath. "I was trimming a hedge in a yard on the street below and when I heard you might need help, I came up here as fast as I could. I saw old Lemondrops running off. Is everything all right?"

"It's all right now," Robin said. "Thanks to Balmy. But how did you know we needed help?"

"Your brother Tommy came hunting for me. He said you and Stella had gone for a walk in the woods and that Mr. Lemon went around the other way after you."

"Tommy?" Robin asked in amazement. "But he wasn't anywhere around when I left. How could he know?"

Julian grinned. "He says he has a scientific way of making himself invisible."

The three young people laughed and Stella wanted to know more about Tommy, whom she had yet to meet.

With Julian they started back toward the Devery house. Since Stella's grandmother would be home soon, it would be better if Stella was there ahead of time.

On the way Julian told her how much his mother liked the dog Stella had modeled in clay. So far he'd had no chance to show it to his father. But he would manage it sometime today.

Robin felt a twinge of envy as she listened. She wished she had made something that might be shown to Mr. Hornfeld, but at the same time she was happy to have Stella's work liked by Julian and his mother.

"I wish I could do something else in clay," Stella said wistfully. "But my grandmother won't let me go to Robin's again."

Robin was tempted to tell her that Mother had a plan in mind, but she held back, lest she raise Stella's hopes without reason. What had happened with Mr. Lemon was a setback, she realized. She should never have lost her temper and said such things to him. He would be sure to use any influence he might have with Mrs. Devery to keep Stella away from the Wards. He would be a real enemy. At the time it had seemed necessary to say something strong enough to save Balmy from harm and to keep Stella from being dragged away against her will.

When they reached the Devery back gate, Robin and Julian waited while Stella crossed the yard. She disappeared through the kitchen door and all was quiet. To Robin it seemed an ominous quiet. There was no telling what might be happening inside.

"Come over to our house for a minute," Julian said. "Mom wants to send something to your mother. She has a good idea."

Robin went with him gladly, and on the way she told him what had happened in the woods.

"Mr. Lemon turned pale when I mentioned the guns to him," Robin said. "He really looked guilty. I don't know what he might have done if Balmy hadn't been there to protect us."

They both laughed together over Balmy behaving as if he were a police dog, but Julian had no further notions about Mr. Lemon and the guns.

At the Hornfelds', Julian's mother was in the kitchen taking a batch of freshly baked brownies out of the oven. "Help yourselves," she invited.

The brownie was delicious and Robin ate it while Julian asked if they could go to his father's studio to get the books.

"Go right out to the studio," Mrs. Hornfeld directed. "He isn't working now—just packing a few things to take to the museum for an exhibit. I spoke to him about the books. Let him choose which ones to send."

The studio door was open, and the two found Mr. Hornfeld putting a marble head into a wooden box nested with straw. When Julian told him what they wanted, he went to a bookshelf and drew out several volumes.

"They're books about blindness," Julian explained. "Dad has quite a few because sometimes he has blind students in his classes. Mom thought you and your mother might like to look through them. Perhaps there

might be a way of lending one of them to Mrs. Devery—
if she is willing to read it."

Robin took the three books Mr. Hornfeld offered her.
The idea was a good one, though she had some doubts
about Mrs. Devery trying to learn anything new.

"Maybe you'd have a minute to look at something,
Dad?" Julian said. He went to a corner shelf where he
had put the board with Stella's clay dog on it, and held
it up for his father to see.

"Stella did this yesterday at the Wards'," he explained. "I told her I wanted to show it to you."

Mr. Hornfeld took the board, turning it about so that
he could study the amusing figure of an exaggerated
Balmy. Robin watched him, feeling as tense as if she
were Stella and about to receive an important verdict.
There was so much kindness in the sculptor's face, so
much sensitivity and understanding. Yet it was a strong
face, too, with an assured look in the eyes and in the set
of the bearded chin. Julian had said his father would
never accept anything second-rate. Whenever Robin
thought of that, her heart sank a notch or two. How
could anything Robin Ward made in clay be anything
but tenth-rate? But every time she set foot in this studio
with its smell of clay and stone and marble dust, the
feeling grew stronger than ever that this was something
she wanted to do.

When the sculptor had examined the small figure
carefully, he nodded his approval. "This is good. It
shows imagination and an understanding of what a dog
is like that goes beyond mere sight. There's texture here
and small details a sighted person might miss unless his
eyes were well trained to observing. Did you say this was
the first thing Stella ever tried in clay?"

Robin shook her head. "She told me she had made a

few things when she lived in Cuba. And yesterday she did something else first." Robin hesitated, not knowing whether she should tell anyone about the lumpy thing Stella had broken up. "She—she didn't keep the other thing she made."

"What was it?" asked Julian.

"I'm not sure. It wasn't anything, really. Just a lot of ugly lumps and angles." What Stella had done worried Robin and she decided to go on. "She said it represented her grandmother and then she took both her fists and smashed it flat. She pounded every bit of it into nothing." Robin couldn't help shivering. "It was awful to watch her."

Julian frowned, but to Robin's surprise Mr. Hornfeld was smiling. "That's what the psychologists call therapy. It's too bad she had to feel so bitter and angry toward her grandmother, but by making something that felt ugly in her hands and punishing it, she undoubtedly got rid of some of the unhappy feelings that were troubling her. I expect she felt better afterward. Less indignant and less resentful. We usually do when we get rid of anger in some physical way that doesn't hurt anyone."

"It's true that she cheered up right away and started making that dachshund," Robin said.

She felt less shivery about Stella's action and she regarded Mr. Hornfeld with increasing admiration.

"I'd like to make a cast of this when it's dry and then a plaster model," he went on. "This girl has an instinctive talent. I'd like to have her in my class sometime."

Again Robin's heart dropped a notch closer to her toes, and the hurtful twinge of envy was there again. It didn't seem fair that Stella should toss off something that interested Mr. Hornfeld so much, while Robin Ward—

"What about you?" Julian's father asked gently. "I presume you were working in clay too?"

His eyes were upon her in a keenly penetrating way, but Robin could not meet his look.

"What I did wasn't any good," she mumbled, and turned hastily toward the door.

Mr. Hornfeld let her go without pushing the matter and Julian came after her. "What did you tell him that for?" he demanded as soon as they were out of the studio.

"Because it's true!" Robin said hotly. "But I don't want to talk about it. I'll take these books home to my mother now."

Julian caught up with her. "Wait a minute. Don't go off in a cloud of steam. You're not being sensible. Yesterday you probably let yourself get tied in knots so your fingers were stiff and wouldn't do what you wanted them to. Perhaps you were a little scared. Stella didn't have any big important goal to worry about. She didn't care, so she went ahead and made any old thing out of clay. Probably it was an accident that it turned out so well. Tomorrow it will go better for you—you'll see."

Robin was too upset to believe what he was saying. "There won't be any chance tomorrow," she told him gloomily. He argued no more, but let her go as she hurried toward home.

On the Ward front lawn Tommy lay on his stomach squinting at something inches away from his nose. Robin was glad to be furnished with a distraction.

"What on earth are you doing?" she asked.

"Studying ants," Tommy said. "When I look at them like this I can be one of them, sort of. I can see how tall the stems of grass are to an ant, and how a clover patch can be a wild jungle."

"At least you're not being invisible," said Robin. "What was that stuff you told Julian about being scientifically invisible?"

Tommy turned over on his back, probably causing consternation to a whole colony of ants. "I was! You know that stack of packing cartons Dad has piled out in the backyard? Well, I was inside the biggest one. I punched holes in the end so I could see everything that was going on in our yard. You didn't see me, did you? So I was invisible."

Robin snorted. "What about spying on Mr. Lemon?"

"I do that all the time," Tommy said cheerfully. "Not out of cartons, but behind trees or under the hedge. I'm not going to tell you all my places. I knew he was going after you and Stella, so I thought I'd better tell Julian."

"I'm glad you did," Robin admitted.

As she carried the books into the house, the sound of her mother's voice on the phone in the back hall reached her. Mother was saying good-by. When she saw Robin, she caught her by the shoulders and whirled her around triumphantly.

"I know how we're going to get through to Mrs. Devery!" she announced. "Come sit down for a minute and I'll tell you about it. That was Mrs. Simpson on the phone."

Mother could be awfully good at stirring up hornets' nests with the most well-intentioned reasons. Robin followed her into the living room. There her mother flung herself full-length on the sofa.

Robin sat on the floor beside her and waited while her mother explained. She found the account hard to understand. It seemed to be mostly past history. About how Agnes—old Mrs. Devery—had been best friends with Edith, whose family had lived in the house that

had been torn down. How Agnes and Edith had visited back and forth during their growing-up years, and Agnes had eventually married Edith's brother Fred, and had one son, Keith—who was Stella's father. After her husband died in the First World War, Agnes became terribly worried about her son. She didn't want him to do anything or go anywhere, for fear something would happen to him. When he started to date girls, she interfered and tried to run his life. Eventually, he got tired of this and he went out west to live for a while. Then he got a good position with an oil company that had an office in Cuba and he moved to Havana. There he married Dolores, and their daughter, Stella, was born.

With some difficulty Robin interrupted this flow. "But, Mother, I know all that. You haven't told me anything new."

"Oh, yes I have!" Mother said. "I can see that you've missed the whole point. But I'm not going through it again."

Robin shook her head as if she were freeing herself from a cobweb of words. None of this seemed helpful when it came to getting Mrs. Devery's permission for Stella to come over to the Wards' every morning.

"What about Mr. Lemon?" she asked. "Does Mrs. Simpson know who he really is?"

"Not under that name," Mother admitted. "But it wasn't your odd Mr. Lemon we were talking about. It was my plan to get past Mrs. Devery's objections so Stella can pose for you again. Mrs. Simpson is going to take care of everything. All we do is wait." She sat up suddenly. "I got so interested, I forgot about lunch. Come and help me put something together."

Out in the kitchen they made large sardine and lettuce sandwiches, one of Mother's favorites. As they worked, Robin told her about the books on blindness Mr. Hornfeld had loaned them. And about his suggestion that they persuade Mrs. Devery to read one of them. Mother thought it a splendid idea, though Robin remained doubtful. With a person who already thought she knew everything, a suggestion that she might have more to learn would not sit very well.

On being called to lunch, Tommy left his scientific studies and joined them at the kitchen lunch counter Dad had put in. Tommy liked sardine sandwiches better than Robin did and he ate three in rather rapid succession without talking. He did listen, however.

Robin was still concerned about Mr. Lemon and she told her mother what had happened in the woods, and of how cross he had been with Stella. Also about that queer thing he had said yesterday concerning guns.

"You must have misunderstood the word," Mother said. "Probably he said something that sounded like guns." And she started to name the words she could think of that rhymed with guns. "Runs, nuns, buns, suns, crumbs, bums—" until Tommy interrupted.

"Guns for Cuba," he said.

Robin and her mother stared at him. Tommy promptly filled his mouth with sandwich so he couldn't talk.

"That's silly," Robin said. "Mr. Lemon is an American. He has nothing to do with Cuba. And old Mrs. Devery doesn't like anything about Cuba."

Tommy chewed for a long while. Then he said, "He speaks Spanish. Spanish with a Cuban pronunciation."

"How do you know that?" Robin asked. "I suppose you were being scientifically invisible again?" She reached out and took the plate away from in front of her brother before he could stuff more food into his mouth.

"You'd better tell us," Mother said. "We don't like to be tantalized."

"I was down the hill at the corner store," Tommy said and took several maddeningly long swallows of milk. "A Puerto Rican woman owns the store, you know, and Mr. Lemon was showing off by giving his order in Spanish. When he went out, I asked her if that's what he was speaking and she said yes, but with a Cuban accent. The way people from different parts of our country speak English in different ways."

"Well!" Mother said, for once completely out of words.

Robin could only regard her brother in admiration. Not even Stella, who lived in the same house with Mr. Lemon, seemed aware that he spoke Spanish. Apparently he had not tried to show off for Stella's mother and had kept his knowledge secret. He must have thought he was safe enough speaking the language outside. But of course he didn't know that Tommy was watching him.

"Guns for Cuba," Mother repeated, puzzling over the words. "But why? From the glimpses I've had of this man, I wouldn't think he'd be given to patriotic causes. And Mrs. Devery wouldn't be either. She's patriotic all right, but her country is old Staten Island. She considers everything else foreign, I'm sure. I'm afraid you're leaping to a pretty big conclusion, Thomas, my son."

"O.K.," Tommy said. "I'll think up something else and let you know."

When the lunch dishes were done, Robin went upstairs and worked for a while with a large lump of clay. She was feeling more relaxed. Julian's words had helped more than she had realized at the time, and she wished she had not walked away from him so ungraciously. Everything had seemed hurtful and discouraging at the moment and she could only think of how Stella had done so easily what she herself could not do.

At last, the shape of a head was developing rather well in the clay. The planes of the cheeks, the slant of the jaw, even the lines of the chin looked right. But she soon realized that she could not do a good likeness from memory. Her imagination could provide her with a wonderful picture. But when she tried to catch its details, the whole thing slipped away. Stella—without sight—had made a creditable dog. It was terribly confusing. When she stopped, however, she did not put the clay back in the tin, but covered it with a damp cloth so she could work on it tomorrow.

The quiet that seemed ominous to Robin continued about the Devery house and grounds until late afternoon. When the telephone rang at the Wards', Robin answered it and went hastily to fetch her mother. Mrs. Devery was calling. Mother listened, spoke politely, and hung up looking slightly dazed.

"This has happened more quickly than I expected," she said. "You and I are invited to have tea with Mrs. Devery on Friday afternoon. This is Mrs. Simpson's doing. She told old Mrs. Devery that I'm interested in Staten Island history—which is perfectly true. But I didn't really expect her to care."

Robin turned a cartwheel down the length of the hall. Once she and Mother were inside the Devery house, with Stella present, they would manage somehow to change old Mrs. Devery's mind. They had to! There was no other way if Robin was to do her head of Stella before the time was up.

(12)

Mrs. Devery Surprises

GLASS WIND-BELLS tinkled as Robin and her mother went up the steps and rang the bell. This time Flora answered the door and invited them into the chandelier-lighted drawing room. A tea table had been set with a lace cloth, and a Chinese bowl filled with pink roses graced the center of it. Mrs. Devery came in wearing her gray silk dress and she behaved more like a hostess this time.

When she had greeted them, she sat at the table and poured tea. Flora carried cups to Mrs. Ward and Robin, and served them sugar and cream or lemon slices from a tray. There were tiny sandwiches and cakes as well—all very appetizing. Mrs. Devery took her own cup and sat again in the fireplace chair beneath her portrait. Though Robin waited anxiously, Stella did not appear.

This time Mrs. Devery gave Mother no chance to chat about anything. Nor did she begin by talking about old Staten Island. Instead she astonished both her visitors by speaking of Mr. Lemon. She was surprisingly frank and wasted no time in getting to the point.

"I was given an account of what happened a few days ago in the woods," she said with a quick glance at Robin. "I understand that your dachshund attacked Harry Lemon quite violently."

156

It was easy to guess who had given her the account. Robin stared at the toes of her shoes and even Mother was momentarily at a loss.

When her visitors said nothing, the old lady went on. Oddly enough, she did not sound particularly indignant. "I have seen Robin's dachshund," she said. "I cannot imagine that he would do any great damage to a grown man."

She managed a slight smile, looking a little more like the picture of the young girl that hung on the wall above her head.

"It's possible," she went on, "that Harry invited the attack by your dog. But it is something else I wish to speak to you about. Apparently my granddaughter and this young lady have picked up some rather dangerous information which they cannot possibly understand. Harry says that Robin threatened to go to the police and report some remark she had overheard concerning guns."

Robin stiffened, no longer interested in her shoes. Her eyes did not leave Mrs. Devery's face. Now, she was sure, would come some sort of fanciful explanation that would go around the truth in order to conceal whatever was important. Again Stella's grandmother surprised her.

"The guns he was speaking of are guns for Cuba," she said.

Robin and her mother exchanged looks. Tommy Ward's correct surmise was incredible.

"I'll explain," Mrs. Devery continued. "Harry—of course Lemon is not his last name—once lived in Cuba. He knew Stella's father, to whom he was related, and he is well acquainted with the men who fought with my son against the dictators. He has been in this underground movement to some extent himself and he knows where guns may be purchased outside of this country and how they may be smuggled to the guerrillas who are still fighting in the mountains of Oriente Province. Money is needed for their purchase and he has come to me for help. I have not decided whether it is wise to invest in this effort. There may be better ways of helping the cause."

Mother spoke impulsively. "How wonderful if you could help a country like Cuba in her fight for freedom!"

"I would not do it for Cuba alone," Mrs. Devery said coldly. "It would be for a cause my dear son believed in and in order to help the friends he loved. Perhaps I owe him this, although I never approved of his living away from Staten Island."

Robin was afraid to speak the suspicions that were crowding up in her own mind and she tried to wigwag signals to her mother by her expression. Apparently the message went through.

"Of course," Mother said, "you would have to be sure of Mr. Lemon. That is, you would have to be sure you were not being tricked."

"Naturally," said Mrs. Devery from a haughty distance. "As I say, Harry is a member of my husband's family. A distant cousin. He has been able to tell me story after story of things I know about that happened in the past. And he knew my son well. He has spent hours telling me about him." Her voice softened. "There is so much I don't know about his years in Cuba."

"I should think your son's wife could tell you more," Mother suggested with her usual lack of diplomacy.

Mrs. Devery turned a look of cold reproach upon her. "This woman is a stranger and a foreigner. I do not wish to discuss family affairs with her."

Mother gasped softly and opened her mouth. She was indignant enough to forget about why they were here, and Robin spoke quickly to save the day.

"Where is Stella?" she asked.

"She will join us presently," said Mrs. Devery. "I wanted to explain this matter of the guns first and ask for your promise to say nothing about it to anyone. If this got around, Harry's entire plan might be endangered, to say nothing of the lives of those who are hiding in Cuba. That is why he is living quietly in my house under an assumed name. It is unfortunate that the matter has leaked out. Since it has, I must trust you. If you will keep silent about this for a little while longer— at least until I make up my mind—I will be deeply in your debt."

Again Robin and her mother exchanged looks.

"Of course we'll promise," Mother said.

Mrs. Devery's nod was regal, as if she expected no less. "Thank you. There is one other thing. Stella is an emotional girl. I don't want her to know the details about this. It would only upset her and bring the sorrow of her father's death uppermost in her mind. I have convinced her that the word she heard the other day was not guns, but gums. Gums from gum-yielding trees. Harry worked on such a plantation at one time and the explanation seemed to fit." She looked directly at Robin. "Will you promise me to say nothing to Stella about the truth?"

Robin squirmed in her chair. She was not as ready to promise as Mother had been. She wanted very much to tell Stella that Mr. Lemon had lived in Cuba and was acquainted with her father. But there seemed nothing to do at the moment but agree. Otherwise she might never be permitted to see Stella again.

"I promise," she said hesitantly.

"Thank you," Mrs. Devery repeated. "I am sure you will keep your word." She relaxed visibly. "Now I'll send for my granddaughter," she said and rang a bell.

Flora went in search of Stella. More tea was poured and the sandwiches and cakes were passed around again.

This was the moment for Mother to produce the book on blindness she had brought with her. "I'd like to lend it to you," she said frankly to Mrs. Devery. "Robin and I have been reading it and we find it helpful in Robin's friendship with Stella. It occurred to me that you might be interested too."

Mrs. Devery had a way of turning unapproachable without saying a word. There was something about her look that shut a door upon whatever offended her. Mother, however, chose not to see the closing door. She went cheerfully on, while Robin held her breath.

"For instance," Mother continued, "I've watched the way you hold Stella's arm when you walk with her. That's the wrong way, you know. The book will tell you how to do it properly. There are all sorts of interesting things to be learned in order to help Stella develop her own independence."

Mrs. Devery flushed, swallowed hard, and murmured that she knew very well how to protect Stella from harm.

Mother said, "Too much protection is the worst thing you can give her. The book will tell you about that too."

It was fortunate that Stella appeared at that moment to halt the discussion. Today she wore an orange-colored skirt and a pink blouse in a screaming combination that set the teeth on edge. She stood in the doorway, not knowing who was in the room, waiting with no smile on her lips.

Mother and Robin said "Hello" to help her out, but her grandmother exploded in disapproval. "Good gracious! What dreadful colors to wear together!"

"How can I tell?" Stella asked sullenly. "You mixed up all my clothes."

"Never mind, never mind," her grandmother said. She rose and took Stella by the arm and led her to a chair that the girl could have found perfectly well by herself. "Sit down and I'll give you some tea."

Robin watched unhappily. She had a feeling that Stella had long since sorted her clothes back into order and that she knew perfectly well what she was wearing. Perhaps she had put these things on to annoy her grandmother.

When Mrs. Devery handed Stella her tea, the girl managed to tip the cup and spill a little into her lap. She groped for a sandwich in a clumsy, helpless sort of way that was not like her. It was as though she were deliberately behaving like the helpless blind girl her grandmother expected her to be.

Mother too sensed that something was wrong. She began to speak animatedly about her talk with Mrs. Simpson. When her neighbor was a little girl, Edith Devery had lived in Catalpa Court. She remembered hearing about the way Agnes and Edith had visited back and forth constantly when they were young.

"Overnight pajama parties were all the rage, I understand," Mother ran on.

Mrs. Devery looked slightly surprised at this digression. "We didn't have pajama parties. We wore nightgowns in those days. But we did love to visit each other. I felt dreadful about seeing the house torn down where my husband and my best friend grew up. I was in that house almost as much as I was in my own home. Now

I understand they are going to build several two-family homes on the lot. The other evening I went over there after the wreckers were gone and poked around idly to see if anything had come through undamaged so I would have a memento. Of course Edith hasn't lived on the island for many years. She married and went south to live and she died a few years ago."

Robin spoke softly, almost afraid to utter the words. "Did you find anything in the wreckage?"

Mrs. Devery's thoughts returned from the past. "As a matter of fact, I did." She went to the whatnot shelves and took down the polished brass incense burner. "This must have been left in the attic when Edith moved and rented the house, so that it fell through to the ground when everything came down. I recognized it at once and brought it home as a reminder of a time when I was very happy. I recall the day Fred took us to an Oriental store over in Manhattan and bought this for his sister. Do you see that bowl on the tea table, with the roses in it?"

Robin and her mother looked at the handsome green bowl. Stella sat still, listening.

"At the same time Fred bought that bowl for me. I'll always remember the day because it was the day he asked me to marry him." She paused, sighing, and Robin suspected that she was talking more to herself than to her visitors. "I am glad I found the incense burner," she finished. But she said nothing about the lid, and Robin did not ask about the thing Stella had told her concerning Mr. Lemon's claim.

There was a silence while Mrs. Devery returned the burner to its place. When she came back to her chair, the moment of sentimentality still lingered.

"Yes," she said, "it's true that Edith and I used to visit each other often. Sometimes we stayed all night at one house or the other."

Mother sprang right in to strike while the iron was hot. "Perhaps your granddaughter would like to repeat the experience that gave you so much pleasure. I wondered if you would let her come and spend the night with Robin sometime?"

Suddenly Robin could see where her mother was heading. She looked at Stella. The girl was eating her sandwich in the messiest way possible, as though she hardly knew where to find her mouth. She could do better than that, Robin felt sure.

In a sense, Mother had placed Mrs. Devery in a corner, but she did not stay there long. "No, I'm afraid not," she said. "The circumstances are quite different. I don't think such a visit would be good for Stella."

"Because I'm blind," said Stella, speaking too loudly and stating the obvious as if she were a small child.

Robin felt a little cross. Stella was putting on an act. No matter how much one might sympathize with Stella's troubles, irritating her grandmother wouldn't help her one bit. Robin forgot to be afraid of Mrs. Devery and spoke her thought aloud.

"You're not as blind as all that!" she told Stella. "If you come to dinner at our house, you can't eat in that messy sort of way."

There was a shocked silence on the part of the two grown-ups. Mother looked as though not even she would have said anything so blunt. Mrs. Devery was clearly outraged. Stella put the last scrap of sandwich in her mouth without any trouble. She wiped her fingers and her mouth neatly. Then she turned her head in Robin's direction and smiled.

"I wouldn't eat like this at your house because you don't expect me to be blind. You don't keep telling me I am."

Mother managed a nervous laugh. "You see?" she said to Mrs. Devery. "I do hope you'll read this book."

Stella turned to her grandmother. "If I can't go over to Robin's, could Robin come here to spend the night sometime soon? We could both work with clay and I could pose for her again. Please, Grandmother."

The look Mrs. Devery turned upon Stella was a strange one, Robin thought. Mingled in it were suffering and despair, pride and confusion, all rolled into one. She didn't hate her granddaughter, Robin thought with sudden clarity. She wanted to love her, but she didn't know how because of those labels Julian had mentioned that were still getting in the way.

"I suppose we could manage that." Mrs. Devery sounded more uncertain than usual. "I can remember how Edith and I—of course you should have a friend, Stella. If Robin's mother is willing, perhaps she could come over and spend the night. Perhaps next Tuesday."

"That would be lovely!" Mother cried, and Stella smiled her warm, bright smile at the three of them.

Mrs. Devery seemed to feel that she must explain something, uncommon though such a gesture was to her. "We do have to look after Stella rather carefully, you know. I've lost all my family. My husband. My son. And Harry Lemon said Stella had a bad fall in the woods Tuesday. I don't want her to be hurt."

"I wasn't hurt, Grandmother," Stella said quickly. "Mr. Lemon never tells the truth. I can tell by voices when people are lying. What he said about my fall being bad wasn't so. He called me a poor little blind girl and I won't be called that! My father said I was a girl like other girls. Robin knows. Robin helps me."

At that moment Julian Hornfeld ran up the steps to the veranda and tapped on one of the long glass doors, having seen them all inside. Mrs. Devery called to him to come in, and he stepped through the open door to bring her an envelope.

"It's a note from my father," he explained. "It's about your portrait."

His eyes turned toward the painting of Agnes Devery as a young girl, and he studied it admiringly as Mrs. Devery excused herself to her guests and read the note. She looked at Julian, puzzled.

"Your father wants to borrow my picture—but I don't understand why. I'm sure I wouldn't want it taken away from the house."

"Will you let him come to see you and explain?" Julian asked. "It's quite important. Important to Staten Island, I mean."

"Well—I suppose so." Mrs. Devery hesitated, perhaps not wanting to agree too easily. "I shall be home next Wednesday morning, if that will do," she said at length.

Julian thanked Mrs. Devery and went out the veranda door as quickly as he had entered.

Mrs. Devery shook her head as though the events of the day had dazed her. Almost as if she spoke to herself, she said the same thing Robin had heard her say once before.

"We never used to have Jewish people in Catalpa Court."

"Isn't it a good thing that there's been a change and Jewish families are willing to mix with Gentiles these days?" Mother said.

Mrs. Devery looked startled. This, clearly, was a

thought that had never occurred to her. Mother went cheerily on.

"One of the things I like about big cities is the way people of different races and religions get to know one another. There's so much we all need to learn. If we only talk to our own kind of people, how can we learn enough in time to live safely in the sort of world we have today?"

Mrs. Devery had endured enough. "I don't like this sort of world," she snapped. "I dislike having strangers come in. I'd prefer everything to be the same as it used to be. We had a much pleasanter, more orderly world when I was young."

"Yet you fought wars because you didn't trust strangers," Mother said relentlessly. "If the countries of Europe had talked to one another a bit more, the way countries talk today, Stella's grandfather might be alive now."

Mrs. Devery was not accustomed to being spoken to like this. She froze as thoroughly as though someone had popped her into the freezing tray of a refrigerator. The tea party was over. But even though she bade Robin and her mother a chilly good-by, the date for an overnight visit was not canceled. Robin was to come over after dinner Tuesday night and stay with Stella. She was to bring her sleeping things, and the clay and tools, and they would once more work together. She hated to wait so long, but she knew nothing could be done about that.

When they were outside the lion gate, Robin looked anxiously at her mother. "Do you think Mrs. Devery understood what you were telling her about people learning from one another? Do you think she'll ever change?"

"I doubt it," Mother said. "People who grow old with

strong prejudices often can't change their way of looking at things. If Mrs. Devery ever accepts the Hornfelds
as friends, she'll probably call them an exception to
what she thinks Jews are like."

"But it's awful if people won't change," Robin said.

"Time changes things," Mother assured her. "The
people who won't change have sons and daughters
growing up, and the sons and daughters have children
of their own. Although you can't talk to the old people
with much success, the younger ones belong to a new
world and sometimes they will listen, and their sons and
daughters will listen. So old prejudices die and there is
change and growth. You young people are the ones who
will make this move faster."

Robin nodded soberly, trying to understand a very
large concept. "Just the same," she said, "there's still
Mr. Lemon, and I don't like him."

"Neither do I," Mother agreed. "I'm worried about
what Mrs. Devery may be getting herself into. In fact, I
wonder if he is even a relative, though she seems convinced that he is. I'm going to talk to your father about
this tonight."

"But you promised not to tell anyone." Robin was
surprised.

"Don't be silly!" Mother said. "Any secrets told to a
wife always get passed along to her husband. Everyone
knows that."

Robin was glad that her father was going to hear
about this. But at the same time, she knew Dad usually
advised not interfering in the affairs of others. Anyway,
she didn't see how it would be possible to tell Mrs. Devery not to do what she was doing.

(13)

Stella's Tunnel

AFTER DINNER on Tuesday, Tommy helped Robin carry her things to the Devery house. Tommy took the overnight bag Mother had lent for the occasion, as well as the big tin of clay. Robin carried the wooden board with the clay head upon it still damp and workable beneath its wet cloth. In the time since Friday she had done more work on the head. She was getting the hair rather well, and the ears were good.

Flora let them in and Mrs. Devery came out of the drawing room to greet Robin and tell her that Flora would take her upstairs to Stella's room. She did not seem to be in a good mood. As she stood in the doorway, Robin could see past her to where Mr. Lemon sat on the sofa, and she wondered if he was the cause of her bad temper. She hoped Dad would decide that something could be done about him, though so far he had only recommended caution.

Tommy handed his load over to Flora and when the woman started upstairs, he whispered to his sister, "Keep away from the dungeon, will you? Those stairs are dangerous."

He went off, leaving Robin to stare after him in astonishment. What on earth was he talking about?

She followed Flora to the front of the third floor where Stella's door stood open, her room unlighted. Flora flicked on the light.

"Sitting in the dark again!" she chided. "Don't you think it's better to act like other people, even if you don't need the light? At least it would make it easier for the rest of us. Here's your company, young lady. Be nice to her now."

Robin liked what she had seen of Flora. She was brusque and stood for no nonsense, but she took a sensible approach when it came to Stella, and did not try to coddle her.

Stella stood in the balcony doorway and turned toward Robin. She was already dressed for the pajama party, wearing blue-striped cotton pajamas instead of the nightgown she had worn the other night. The emerald and diamond pin was fastened boldly to her collar.

"Did you bring the clay?" she asked eagerly. "Flora fixed a card table for us and left some old oilcloth we can spread over it. And she gave me a chopping board just like yours."

Robin set her burden down on the table and looked around. Stella's room was a good deal larger than Robin's. The ceiling was high and the thinly shaded bulb hanging from its center cast a harsh, unpleasant light. Probably Mrs. Devery didn't think it mattered, since Stella couldn't see it anyway. Otherwise, the room was pleasantly furnished with a highboy and a bureau which were probably antiques. There was a drop-front desk and a big comfortable armchair, as well as two or three straight chairs. The bed was huge and made of dark-reddish mahogany with a big headboard. Robin noted that everything was neatly placed. None of the

chairs jutted carelessly into the room, so that Stella was able to move about easily, locating familiar landmarks with her elbow, or toe, or the back of her hand. On the bureau her brush and comb and other toilet articles were laid out exactly, and Robin knew that Stella must have placed them in a pattern that enabled her to find what she wanted without hesitation. In many ways Stella was able to live quite comfortably within the boundaries of her own four senses. It was only when sighted people expected the wrong things of her, or did not expect enough of her, that there seemed to be trouble.

Stella seemed pleased and excited over Robin's visit. "Put your pajamas on right away," she said. "Perhaps we can work with your clay for a while before it's time for bed."

Robin began to unpack in the area on the far side of the bed that Stella indicated was to be hers. On a shelf near the bed stood a lovely wooden statue of Mary and her baby son that caught Robin's eye.

"Your statue," she said, "—it must be hand-carved?"

Stella took the figure from the shelf. Her fingers moved lightly over the dark, glossy wood. "Yes, it is. Manuel, the father of our gardener in Havana, was a fine wood-carver. He made this for me when I was small because he said I couldn't touch the large figures in our church and I must know what the baby Jesus and his mother were like."

This seemed a beautiful thought to Robin. Sometime soon Stella must visit Mr. Hornfeld's studio and see with her sensitive fingers the series of heads he was doing.

When Robin had unpacked, leaving nothing where Stella might stumble over it, she put on her own red-

and-white polka-dot pajamas—a joke present from
Tommy last Christmas. She and Stella spread out their
tools on the covered top of the card table. Robin was
eager to continue work on the clay head. Somehow she
had a feeling that things might come along better for
her.

At first the girls did not talk, intent upon getting
started. Here in this high room sounds reached them
from a distance, hardly disturbing the quiet. A faraway
radio could be heard, and a jet plane from Newark Airport went over high above. From the veranda below
came the faint, light sound of wind-bells. Inside the
room a clock ticked loudly in the silence.

Robin looked around to locate it and saw that a large
old-fashioned alarm clock stood on Stella's bureau. She
found its presence puzzling.

"When you have a Braille watch, why do you need a
clock?" she asked.

"For the sound it makes," Stella explained. "I can
always locate myself by the ticking. Just the way I get
around Grandmother's living room by listening to that
prickly clock on the mantel."

"Prickly" was a good word for the gilt mantel clock
with its spikes and curlicues, Robin thought. She was
working now in an effort to finish Stella's feathery cap
of hair and straight bangs in the clay. She concentrated
for a while without talking, turning the head from time
to time, or standing up to walk around Stella. The effect
was coming quite well, so she could postpone the face
for a while longer.

Stella too was shaping a head out of the big lump of
clay on her own board. She had already run her hands
lightly over the head Robin was doing, and now she was
forming a similar shape.

"I'm going to do Mr. Lemon," she announced, and there was a sound of mischief in her voice. "Today I found out what Grandmother believes about the lid to the incense burner. I asked about it and she said it was something Mr. Lemon had picked up from the family years ago. Since it didn't match anything, he kept it for a lucky piece. When Grandmother found the rest of the burner, he decided to give it to her. Of course this has convinced her all the more that he is a relative."

Robin gasped. "Did you tell her that what he said isn't true?"

"Not yet. I have to wait for the right time, so she'll believe me, instead of him."

Stella went on patting at the clay, forming fat cheeks like Mr. Lemon's.

"How can you tell what he looks like?" Robin wondered.

Stella's laughter was faintly malicious. "This evening I had a good chance. He was lying on Grandmother's brocade sofa—where she doesn't like him to be. I could tell by his snoring that he was asleep. He even had his feet right up on the brocade. I felt for them. He was on his back and I leaned over him and put both my hands on his face and held him down for a minute."

Robin regarded her in horror. "What did he do?"

"He yelped as if I were going to murder him and flew right up in the air. I think I gave him a real scare. He came after me and I don't know what he'd have done if he had caught me. But I can move faster than he can, and I went through the door and out into the hall. Grandmother was coming down the stairs and when he saw her he stopped trying to catch me. Of course she wanted to know what had happened. He told her I'd tried to strangle him. He said I was becoming dangerous."

Robin felt increasingly shocked. "She didn't believe that, did she?"

"Of course not. She has some sense. I put on my best dumb-little-blind-girl act and said I only wanted to know what he looked like. And how could I tell unless I touched him? But I think he'll try to get even with me now."

Robin shook her head. "I think you're pretty awful sometimes. I think you take advantage of being blind."

"Why shouldn't I? I get so tired of the way people treat me—being sorry for me, not really liking me!"

Robin thought about this for a minute. "Maybe some of that is because they don't know any better. Maybe some of it's your fault. Part of the time I like you, and part of the time I don't. Maybe if you want people to like you, you have to give them something to like. My father says there isn't any other way. But I know it's hard. Sometimes when I'm mad enough I don't care whether anybody likes me or not."

Stella bent her head over the clay and the blank, on-guard look kept her thoughts secret. Robin knew it was time to change the subject.

"Do you wear your star pin to bed?" she asked.

Stella's head came up defiantly. "Of course! Grandmother says good night downstairs, so she doesn't know. And my mother doesn't mind."

"But why? I should think the points might prick you at night."

"It keeps me out of tunnels," Stella said. "Tunnels where there's only me and—and a sort of nothingness. I used to get the tunnel feeling sometimes when I was little. Maybe because we had to crawl through a long tunnel once when there was danger and my father was afraid the soldiers were coming for us. It was an awful feeling with those tight sides pushing in all around—as if I might be crushed under the ground any minute. Afterward, I used to dream about it at night and wake up crying. That was when my *abuela* gave me the emerald star. She said I had only to touch it to know that the night sky went on and on up there—all the way to God. And I had the whole big world around me to move about in. She said when I touched the star pin I would know that I was part of a whole universe and I had been put here for a reason. Even if I didn't understand what the reason was, I would *know*."

Robin reached out to touch Stella lightly on the hand. "I think I know what you mean. Tell me what Cuba was like."

As they worked, Stella talked, bringing back from memory the sweet scent of flowers, the sound of waves rushing up to break on the rim of a beach, the cool smell of the mountains when the mists came down, the feeling of languorous heat in the city. The sounds of busy Havana streets too, and the night sounds—often of people singing. She remembered some of the Spanish songs and she sang snatches of them in a voice that Robin thought heartbreakingly beautiful.

She was singing when her grandmother walked into the room and stood looking about critically, as though eager to find something wrong. Stella heard her step at once and was silent. The two growing clay heads did not interest Mrs. Devery, but her eyes rested at once on the pin Stella wore on the collar of her pajamas. At once she bore down on her granddaughter and unfastened the catch before Stella knew what she was about.

"I've had enough of this!" Mrs. Devery said, stepping back with the pin in her hand. "Wearing it on cotton dresses! Even on your pajamas! And Harry has told me that you were wearing it in the woods the other day too. I'm going to put it away in my jewel box, where it will be safe. I shall keep it for you until you are old enough to appreciate its value and treat it with the proper respect."

She turned angrily and went out of the room, leaving Stella sitting stricken before her mound of clay.

"She doesn't understand," Robin whispered. "Perhaps if I explained to her about your Cuban grandmother—"

Stella seemed not to hear. She left her chair and followed the ticking clock across the room till the back of her hand touched the bed. She climbed onto it and sat in the middle, with her arms clasped about her knees, and began to rock from the waist, back and forth, back and forth, there on the bed. Her blank, guarded look and the rocking motion were somehow frightening to see. Robin sensed that Stella had returned to that tunnel of her own accord and the world had faded away from around her. It was as if she were the only living thing left, and her rocking told her that she was at least alive.

Robin had no idea what to do or say. She thought of going after Mrs. Devery and calling her back to see the result of what she had done. But before she could move toward the door, Stella's mother came running down the hall and into the room.

She stood in the doorway and took in the scene at a glance.

"Her grandmother took the star pin," Robin whispered.

"Yes, I know this," young Mrs. Devery said. "I have

seen her just now in the hall." Her dark eyes filled with tears as she watched Stella rocking on the bed. "She does not do this since she is a small child. It is terrible."

Robin remembered the first scene she had beheld in this room, glimpsed from her balcony at home. She remembered the loving gesture her mother had made toward Stella, and the way the girl had turned away. The same scene seemed about to be repeated and she sensed that this was deeply wounding to Stella's mother, and hurtful to Stella as well.

"Make her stop," she whispered to Mrs. Devery. "Can't you make her stop?"

The Cuban woman blinked hard to free her vision of tears. She went to the bed and took hold of Stella's shoulders. "Stop it!" she commanded, sounding less gentle. "Stop it at once! Your father would never allow such a thing. You know that, Estrellita."

It was the mention of her father that stopped the rocking. Stella hunched up her knees and hid her face against them.

Relentlessly, her mother went on. "Blind children do this at one time or another. But whenever you started to rock, your father would stop you because he did not wish you to grow up and make a spectacle of yourself in a world that can see. Rocking is only for babies."

Stella relaxed and sudden tears rolled down her cheeks. "I was in the tunnel again," she mourned. "Without my star I'm nothing, nobody."

Robin leaned on the end of the bed and spoke her mind. "That's silly. That is being a baby. What your grandmother gave you was an idea to hold on to. The things you told me about are there, reaching all the way up to the sky. You don't need the pin to tell you that."

Mrs. Devery smiled at Robin through the tears in her eyes. "You hear, my Estrellita? What your American friend says—this is true. There are no such tunnels here in America."

"I hate my grandmother!" Stella cried. But at least she was no longer rocking. She rolled off the bed, away from her mother's reaching hands, and found her way back to the card table. "I want to work at this clay," she said.

Her mother watched for a long worried moment. She managed a quavery smile for Robin and slipped from the room.

"She has gone?" Stella said.

"She's gone," Robin told her. "She was crying. You've hurt her feelings badly."

"What about my feelings?" Stella demanded. "I'm the one who has been hurt!"

"Not only you," Robin said a little fiercely. Somehow she had to get through to Stella and make her understand. "Other people can be hurt too. Your mother and your grandmother. Mr. Lemon when you frightened him tonight. Though I'm not worried about him. You can't go on thinking you're the only one in the world with feelings, or you'll never grow up."

Stella paid no attention. Her hands were upon the clay again. "I'm going to make Mr. Lemon's face the way it felt under my fingers—fat and ugly. When I get it made, I'm going to mash it flat and roll it into nothing."

Robin remembered Mr. Hornfeld's words in time and managed not to shiver. "Good for you!" she said. "When you've done that you won't feel so angry with everyone."

Stella looked startled, as if she had expected further disapproval. She went furiously to work on the clay.

Robin returned to the head of Stella, which was beginning to take on a likeness beneath her fingers. Now she was ready to try the face. It was as if some inner power guided her, some inner confidence she had never known before, and she worked quickly, skillfully. But what was appearing in the clay wasn't Stella's bright, smiling expression that had so charmed Robin in the beginning. Instead, it was the sad, uncertain Stella who sometimes looked out from behind the smile. If she could catch this uncertain expression as she had seen it, perhaps it would say something about Stella to other people. Perhaps her work would make them understand her better.

Robin's fingers moved quickly and surely.

(14)

The Clay Takes Shape

THE PAJAMA PARTY had ended by being fun. The girls had worked for a while longer on the two clay heads. Stella's piece did not look much like Mr. Lemon, but it was definitely puffy and fat. Robin had managed to get a fairly good nose on her piece, and the mouth and contours of the cheeks were almost perfect. Somehow, in a way she did not understand, she had caught the sad little half-smile, the look of hesitancy and doubt—as if the clay girl did not know exactly what to expect from the world. The chin was coming well too, and the form of the lower face. She had started on the bony structure of the brows, but as yet she had not touched the eyes. Perhaps they would be the most difficult to do well. Not that Stella's eyes seemed so different from other people's. They were remarkably lifelike and moved naturally. But eyes were always difficult, and these needed the faraway look Stella sometimes seemed to wear, perhaps because there was no real focus in her eyes.

When Stella's mother came in to tell them it was bedtime, both girls smiled at her more happily. She tucked them into the big bed and kissed them both good night. They lay beneath light summer covers, whispering for a while, and then grew drowsy and fell asleep.

When Robin wakened, a long bar of sunshine from the balcony door fell across the mahogany bed and for a moment she couldn't think where she was. She rolled over to speak to Stella and found that the other girl was already up and out of the room.

She drowsed for a few moments and thought pleasantly of the clay head that had begun to come right last night. An urgency came to her to see it by daylight and find out if what had seemed good before she went to sleep would still be so in the morning. She slipped out of bed and ran barefoot to the card table where the clay heads stood protected by their damp coverings. She was almost afraid to look as she pulled the cloth from the clay face.

It was true! She had begun to catch something that was like Stella. The expression of the mouth was right— it *was* Stella! Robin had never felt so great an elation, or a satisfaction so intense. At that moment what anyone else thought of her work didn't matter. *She* knew it was good and she had done it with her own hands and out of her own creative ability. Even if the eyes never came right, she knew she had achieved something—something worth showing to Mr. Hornfeld. But she would not let him see it until the whole thing was finished to the best of her ability.

She could see that the cleft of the chin needed a touch more work and she moved the card table so that the bar of sunlight would give her the best possible lighting. She shaped and changed and improved the chin a little.

She had finished and gone back to the bed when Stella came into the room, still in her pajamas. She looked excited, as if having a visitor overnight was something she was not used to.

"If you're awake," she said, "the bathroom's empty. Grandmother has hung up towels for you on the left-hand rack, and I guess I won't need to show you where the paper and the soap are."

"Of course not," Robin said, puzzled. She put on her slippers and got her toothbrush from the overnight case.

"I forgot you can see," Stella said, sensing her astonishment. "A strange bathroom can be the hardest room in a house for a blind person. I've spent ages hunting for things because no one showed me where they were located, and every bathroom is different."

Here was another aspect of blindness she had not considered, Robin thought as she went down the hallway to a door that opened into an old-fashioned bathroom. The tub stood high upon claw feet and the faucets did not mix the water. The plug was enormous and hung on a long brass chain.

She hurried a bit with her morning washing, eager to have breakfast and get back to her work on the clay head. The work drew her as nothing else had ever done. This was not like the piano-playing. This was something she wanted, that she yearned to do better. To have Mr. Hornfeld as a teacher would give her so much that she needed to improve. If the head of Stella kept on growing as it had done so magically last night, she knew she would have something worth showing him. Not professional, of course, but something that would surely make him want her in his class.

There were other reasons to hurry as well. Last night she had seen nothing of Mr. Lemon, but he would be around this morning and perhaps something would come of being in the same house with him. Something she might tell Dad which would help in his judgment of what to do to keep Mrs. Devery out of trouble. That matter of the incense burner lid was important, but there ought to be more.

She saw nothing of him at breakfast, however. He seemed to have retreated into hiding as he did when anyone from outside came in. Mrs. Devery apparently got up early and had already eaten and gone on an errand in her car. Stella's mother had left for work earlier. When the two girls came downstairs, Flora fixed them a breakfast of pancakes and sausages which they ate at a table in the big kitchen.

Stella ate very neatly this morning. Now and then she touched the rim of her plate so she could be sure she wasn't moving food over the edge. Sometimes she used a bit of toast to help her locate what was there. Flora cut up the sausage for her, but otherwise she needed no help and she did not repeat Friday's performance when she had been deliberately trying to annoy her grandmother by eating untidily.

This morning she seemed keyed up and a bit triumphant. Robin began to feel that her mood grew from something more than the fact that she was enjoying the company of a guest. It was as if Stella had some scheme at the back of her mind that excited her, and Robin wondered uneasily what she might be planning.

Flora was pleased that they were both hungry and she gave them as many pancakes as they could manage. When they were through, Stella made a suggestion.

"It's going to be another hot day, so let's move our things downstairs to the big veranda. If there's a breeze, we'll find it there and we can have an outdoors feeling while we work—the way we did at your house. My balcony's too small, and we'd be crowded there."

Robin thought this a good idea, and they hurried upstairs to bring down the two clay heads. Stella went to the card table and picked up Robin's board. Robin would have preferred to carry it herself, but the head was protected by a cloth, and she knew Stella would be careful. She picked up the second board and followed Stella downstairs. Inside the house, where the other girl knew her way around, she did not need to hold anyone's arm. She managed well on the stairs, moving with the banister at her elbow as a guide. She knew the number of steps, where the bend came, and where to put her feet.

The veranda ran across the front of the house and around on the same side that faced toward the Wards'. They set the two heads down on the veranda floor and Robin went back upstairs for the folding card table.

In a few minutes she had it set up in the place where the veranda turned, so they could get a breeze from two directions. Morning glory vines shaded them from the direct sun, and there was plenty of light for Robin's work.

When the table was ready, Stella again picked up the board Robin was working on, carried it to her place at the table, and sat down before it. To Robin's distress, she peeled off the cloth, picked up an orangewood stick, and reached toward the head.

"That's my work!" Robin cried. "Here, let me put yours in front of you."

Stella dropped the stick, her hands searching the clay until she was sure she had made a mistake and picked up the wrong head. The error seemed to worry her.

"But I couldn't have taken the wrong one," she said. "I know where I put it when I brought it down. I know which one I picked up."

"You carried mine downstairs to start with," Robin said. "You made the mistake up in your room."

"How could I? I knew which side of the table I was working on. I know I picked up the right one."

Robin remembered. "I turned the table around this morning while you were out of the room," she explained sheepishly. "I got out of bed to see how my piece looked. I wanted to add something to the chin and I moved the table toward the light."

Stella's anger flared quickly. "Don't you know any better than that? Don't you know that you mustn't switch things around so that I can't find something where I left it? You ought to have better sense!"

"Well, don't get so mad about it," Robin said. "I know I shouldn't have moved the table without telling you. But I forgot and there's no harm done. Let's go on with what we're making."

"I don't want to," Stella said crossly. "I don't like what I was making anyway." With both hands she began to tear apart the clay head Robin had put before her. When this seemed difficult, she took the blunt knife and chopped the clay into small pieces. Then she stuck it together again and rolled it into long snakes. These she hung about her neck one after another, as if she were putting on necklaces. She still looked furiously angry, and Robin decided to ignore her and go on with her own work.

"I want to go on with mine, if I can," she said. "The face is coming right now. I'm beginning to catch the way you looked last night. The way you look now is no help to me."

Stella scowled still more deeply. "Let me see," she snapped. She reached toward Robin's clay piece and Robin watched anxiously, ready to snatch her hands away if Stella did any harm. But she merely touched the head lightly, looking at it with her fingers in her own way. The anger seemed to drain out of her.

"Is that really the way my mouth is?" she asked, tracing the clay lips with a gentle finger and then touching her own mouth.

"Sometimes," Robin said.

The searching fingers moved along the chin and over the smoothly rounded cheeks toward the eye sockets above. "There's nothing here," Stella said, "You haven't finished the eyes."

She began to poke and prod at the clay, spoiling the shape of one brow and Robin slapped her hands away indignantly. "Don't do that! You're spoiling it. This is the best thing I've ever done and I won't have it damaged. I need it to show to Mr. Hornfeld. How can you be so mean?"

Stella's hands fell away from the clay and her lips trembled. She looked as if she were about to burst into tears. Before Robin could say anything more, she turned away and walked along the side veranda to the place where steps ran down to the yard. She put a hand on the rail and went down them, still wearing her wriggly necklaces of clay.

Robin did not follow her. She felt thoroughly annoyed with Stella's behavior. She wasn't going to chase after her. She wanted to work on her clay, and that was what she meant to do. Blind or not, Stella ought to grow up and stop behaving like a baby.

Robin went to work repairing the slight damage Stella had done to the brow above one eye socket. Then she began to work on the shape of the eyes. From the clay Stella's mouth smiled at her in a half-sad, half-hesitant way, looking not at all as Stella had looked just now. Yet the angry look was Stella too, and it haunted Robin until she gave up her futile attempt to get at least one of the eyes right. She put the damp cloth over the clay and went down the back steps in search of Stella.

The yard stood empty. There was no telling where Stella had gone. Robin hoped it was not into the woods by herself.

"Psst! Psst!" came a hiss from nearby.

Robin jumped and looked toward the hedge between the Devery yard and the Wards'. Her brother's head poked through a newly made hole in a rear section of the hedge.

"If you're looking for Stella," he whispered, "she's gone down to the dungeon." He waggled a finger, pointing.

Robin saw that the Devery cellar door at the side of the house stood open. She looked inside. There was a small entryway, with stairs straight ahead that led up to the kitchen. A second flight on her right dropped away into the darkness of the cellar. From Tommy's gesture, she gathered that it was down this steep, dark flight that Stella had gone. Gingerly, Robin felt her way down three steps, clinging to the rail. A musty smell of mildew and dampness came up to her. The furnaces and water heater must be in another part of the cellar. This part smelled long unused. No wonder Tommy called it a dungeon. It was hard to believe that Stella was down there alone.

She called her name a bit fearfully. Below, everything remained dark and quiet. But the door to the kitchen flight opened at the top, and Mr. Lemon stood looking down at Robin. He gave her a smile as sour as his name.

"If you're looking for Stella, she's down there sulking," he told her. "There's no use calling her. She'll sit there until she's ready to come up, or until her grandmother tells her to."

Robin, looking down into chill blackness, could only shudder. She was certainly not going down into that awful place to search for Stella. Nor did she want to stay here listening to Mr. Lemon. She went quickly outside and returned to the veranda. The morning was going badly. Stella's behavior had upset and distracted her, and it was hard to give wholehearted attention to the work Robin needed to do. Nevertheless, she must try. Already the first of September seemed to be rushing toward her too quickly.

Perhaps she could form the eyes in the clay face as if the lids were closed. That might be easier to do than to represent them as open. Having the eyes closed might indicate blindness in a symbolic sort of way. She wished Stella were here so she might see how her eyelids fell when her eyes were closed. Since she wasn't, Robin went determinedly to work to get this effect right by herself. Before long she was once more so absorbed in her work that it was as if the rest of the world was shut out. There was no thought in her mind except what was happening to the clay beneath her fingers.

So deep was her concentration that she was startled when she heard footsteps on the walk. She looked up to see Mr. Hornfeld coming toward the front steps. She had forgotten that he was supposed to visit Mrs. Devery this Wednesday morning. Robin knew her work would be perfectly visible to him as he came up the steps and she moved swiftly, patting the damp cloth over the head, hiding it from view.

"Good morning," Mr. Hornfeld said. He must have seen her hasty gesture, but he made no comment. "Do you know if Mrs. Devery is about?"

"She went out in the car," Robin said, wishing she wouldn't blush so guiltily. "I expect she'll be home soon, since she knew you were coming."

"I'll sit down, if I may," the sculptor said and seated himself in a cane chair near the card table. "I see I've interrupted your work. Why don't you go on with it?"

Robin shook her head. "I'm through for now." Since he was here at hand and not busy, she could not resist asking a question. "Are most of the submissions for your young people's class in?" she inquired.

"Almost all. But I wait until the first of September to make a decision. There are quite a few pieces coming in this year. I wish I could manage two classes, but with my adult teaching at the museum and my own work besides, there's not enough time. It's not a good idea, for me at least, to work with too many in a class. The personal attention I can give is the important thing. So I want to choose those who can most benefit by the class."

Robin could feel the familiar sinking sensation again. How could she hope that this head of Stella would be good enough to justify her entry into his class?

"Does every student in the class have to bring a finished piece?" she persisted, though she knew the answer very well.

Mr. Hornfeld nodded. "Yes, since this helps me to judge each applicant's work, and it also gives each person in the class something to compete with, to improve on."

"What if someone does something good just by luck—and can't ever do it again?"

Mr. Hornfeld's dark eyes were understanding. "This can happen to all of us. By great good fortune we may happen to get everything right without knowing how we did it. That's what inspiration can sometimes do. And it's why any creative worker needs to learn his craft. He must know how to use his tools, instead of depending on anything so uncertain as inspiration alone. I like what a famous French artist used to tell his own students. 'First of all learn to be a good craftsman. This will never keep you from being a genius.' "

"But I should think anyone could learn the craft part," Robin pondered.

"Almost anyone can learn to go through the motions. But there's something else about creative work that we can't pin down. For want of a better word we call it talent. It means that extra something—the natural bent a person has toward one sort of work or another. The person who has a strong bent in one direction is fortunate. If he's willing to work and to learn, he will probably succeed."

Robin sighed deeply. "My mother says I never finish what I start. But when I see that something isn't turning out as well as I want it to, I get discouraged. It doesn't seem worthwhile going on."

Mr. Hornfeld studied her for a moment as if he could guess very well what lay hidden beneath the damp cloth. "If this continues to be true as you grow older, I would feel sorry for you. It's much better to finish badly than not to finish at all. It seems to me that only the persistent ones who keep coming back again and again after disappointment can deserve success."

Robin thought about that, thought about the hidden clay. This time she would finish. Perhaps she would finish well. Her confidence in what lay hidden beneath the cloth was returning.

A step on the veranda behind her made Robin turn. Stella had come up the back steps. Her blouse was torn, and there was a black smudge across one cheek. Her hands were dirty, and there were cobwebs in her hair.

"Good morning," said Mr. Hornfeld pleasantly, as if not in the least surprised by her appearance.

Stella returned his greeting in an absentminded way, clearly thinking of something else. In her soiled hands she was carrying a wad of clay. Apparently, sitting down there in musty darkness, she had wadded the long snakes back into a whole piece again. As she set the lump down on the card table, Robin saw that dirty fingerprints had been pressed into the clay.

"I don't know what to do," Stella said in the same absent voice. "I just don't know what to do."

Before Robin could ask what she meant, Mrs. Devery's car turned into the driveway. She braked to a stop and started to get out, carrying a large bag of groceries. At once Mr. Hornfeld went to help her. Under cover of this distraction, Stella whispered hurriedly to Robin.

"Is the clay head you're doing of me any good, Robin? Do you think Mr. Hornfeld will accept it?"

The urgency in her tone was surprising.

"I don't know," Robin said. "I can't tell by myself. I hope it is."

"Show it to him," Stella urged. "Show it to him now. Let him see it before he goes home today."

"I don't want to," said Robin firmly. "It's not ready yet. The eyes aren't finished. And I want to go over everything and see that it's smooth and right."

"You're afraid to show it to him," Stella challenged. "You're afraid he won't think it's good enough."

That was probably true, Robin thought, but still she would not be hurried. She had ten days or more until September first to get it as right as she could make it. It would be silly to turn it in before she was satisfied that she could do no more.

"I want to wait," she said stubbornly.

Stella brushed her hands across her face as though she brushed cobwebs away, leaving further smears of grime behind. "I don't know what to do," she repeated, thinking again of her own problems.

Mrs. Devery came up the steps, with Mr. Hornfeld following, carrying the grocery load. At once her eyes fell on the disheveled Stella.

"You've been in the old cellar again!" she cried. "Why must you go down to that dirty place when I've asked you not to?"

Stella turned defiantly toward her grandmother's voice. "No one can stare at me down there. I can be alone. I can think without anyone interrupting me."

Mrs. Devery raised her eyebrows at Mr. Hornfeld and shrugged in a despairing manner. Flora came to the front door and took the bag of groceries from Mr. Hornfeld. He and Mrs. Devery sat in chairs on the veranda. The old lady was upset and not in a good mood.

"You wanted to speak to me about the portrait painted of me when I was a girl?" she asked Mr. Hornfeld curtly.

"I certainly do," he told her. "But if you don't mind, I'd like to show your granddaughter something first."

From the pocket of his jacket he took the amusing little dachshund Stella had made. It had been repro-

duced in plaster, and the finished piece was astonishingly good. He put it into Stella's hands, and she ran her fingers over the white, slightly rough surface, examining every detail. She set it down on the card table, well in from the edge, without saying a word.

"May I show it to your grandmother?" Mr. Hornfeld said, and picked up the piece.

Stella remained silent, as if the matter no longer interested her. Mrs. Devery examined the dog in some amazement.

"You mean Stella made this?"

"She made the clay model. It's very good, isn't it?" Mr. Hornfeld said. "If Stella is interested in joining my class, she could use this as an entry piece. I've had some

remarkably talented blind children in other classes of mine. Of course, as I was telling Robin, I can't make a final decision until I've seen all the pieces submitted to me."

"I don't want to be in your class," Stella said, sounding as though tears were not far away. "I don't ever want to make anything out of clay again!"

She rose and found her way into the house. The screen door slammed behind her.

"I apologize for my granddaughter's bad manners," said Mrs. Devery stiffly.

"You needn't," Mr. Hornfeld assured her. "I have daughters of my own. She may feel different about this by tomorrow. But now may I ask for the loan of your portrait during the last two weeks of September? We are planning a museum exhibit of the art of former days, all done by Staten Island artists. I have been told that your portrait is an outstanding piece of work, and the exhibition will not be complete without it. I can assure you that the picture will be treated with great care and returned to you safely."

Mrs. Devery appeared for once to be caught off guard. Perhaps she felt that she could not refuse flatly in the face of Mr. Hornfeld's kindness and her granddaughter's rude behavior.

"Would you like to see the portrait?" she asked and rose to lead the way into the house.

When they had gone inside, Robin went quietly through the front door and ran upstairs. She would go to Stella's room and pack her things and go home. There was nothing else to do.

(15)

In the Dungeon

WHEN ROBIN went upstairs to pack, she found Stella lying across her bed weeping. There was no comfort Robin could offer, and she said quietly that she was going home.

Stella's choked voice came from the depths of her pillow. "When you go, take that clay head with you. I don't want to pose for you anymore. Don't leave it here. I—I might do something to it."

"Whatever is the matter?" Robin demanded. "What is it that's worrying you?"

"I can't tell you." Stella's voice was half muffled. "Just go home and don't ask any more questions."

Robin had no intention of leaving her precious clay head behind. She was so close to finishing it that it no longer mattered whether Stella posed or not. Nevertheless, she felt unhappy about behavior she could not understand. She was worried for Stella on her own account.

"Why do you behave the way you do?" she asked helplessly. "Why do you push people away when they only want to be friends?"

"Nobody wants to be friends with a blind girl!" Stella wailed. "And anyway, you don't understand. You don't understand at all!"

197

"I certainly don't want to be friends with you the way you are now," Robin said, flinging pajamas and slippers into her mother's overnight case. "But that hasn't anything to do with your being blind."

Stella wept without answering and she did not reply when Robin tried stiffly to thank her for the invitation and said good-by.

During the several days after that distressing scene, nothing was heard from the Devery house. Mrs. Devery called Julian over to do some transplanting, and the holes in the hedge were plugged with new growth. Robin could still look down into the grounds from the upstairs windows of the Ward house, but except for glimpses of Flora, Mrs. Devery, and Mr. Lemon, the place was quiet. Stella remained out of sight.

Dad continued to advise waiting as far as Mr. Lemon was concerned. The matter was solely Mrs. Devery's business and one could not make suggestions to her unasked, he pointed out.

One morning Robin sent a message across in the basket from her balcony to Stella's and tinkled the far bell. But no one came out and the message remained unclaimed beneath the stone weight. Robin began to wonder if Stella might be ill.

From Julian she heard that Mrs. Devery had agreed to lend her famous portrait for the museum exhibit. When she had the opportunity, Robin told him the whole story of her curious visit to Stella's. But she would not show Julian or anyone else the clay head that was finished and drying. Only Mother had seen it. She had used the direct method of taking the cover off and looking. It had been encouraging to hear her response.

"Why, this is good!" she cried. "Robin honey, this is

awfully good. Let's call Dad and show it to him right
away."

Robin had promptly opposed that. "Not yet. I don't
want anyone to see it yet."

She felt uncertain about her work, sometimes hopeful, sometimes doubtful. Although Mother knew a lot
about working in clay, her standards were probably for
the lower grade school level of the younger children she

was accustomed to teaching. Robin was still afraid to submit the head to a final test until the very last minute.

Then came a gray and misty day when Mother was giving an afternoon tea for some of her new friends in Catalpa Court. They had been kind about inviting her to their homes, and she wanted to give them a special party. The house was in a bustle most of the day, with baking going on and little sandwiches being made by the score. Robin was pressed into helping part of the time, but Tommy made himself invisible and was never around when he might have been useful.

Mrs. Devery had been invited, but she had written a note to regret that she had to go to Manhattan on the day of the tea.

When mists rolled in from the bay and settled on Staten Island, the hilltops were lost in fog and the very outlines of the hills faded into the sky. There was no rain, but a thick gray mist hung over everything, wiping out all but the nearest colors.

In spite of the mist, it was a noisy, ear-shattering afternoon, and not wholly because of Mother's party. A bulldozer had arrived that morning to start excavating for the new houses that were to be built in the place where Edith Devery had once lived. Mother was distressed because of the uproar it made, but since her visitors lived in the court, they would understand.

When the guests began to arrive, Robin escaped to her own room and spent some time studying the head she had done of Stella Devery. The clay was about dry now and perhaps if Mr. Hornfeld found it good enough —But she hardly dared think of that.

As she sat in her room, a sound near enough at hand to make itself heard in spite of outside noises reached her. The bell on her balcony had tinkled. Robin ran outside and looked through misty treetops toward Stella's room. There was no one in sight. The basket had not been returned, and when she pulled it across she found nothing under the stone weight except the unclaimed note she had put there.

She jerked Stella's bell inquiringly, but for a moment nothing happened. She could just make out Stella's glass door, and it seemed to her that one of its small panes had been broken. While she considered this strange fact, a hand appeared in the open space and flung something through it. The object sailed over the balcony rail, missed the basket, and dropped into the Devery yard. Something was certainly wrong and Robin wasted no more time.

She hurried downstairs and out of the back door. Without respect for Mrs. Devery's hedge repairs, she thrust her way through the weakest spot and crawled into the other yard. Something white lay on the ground below Stella's balcony. Robin picked it up and saw that a filing card had been folded around another one of Stella's polished stones and fastened with a rubber band.

Opening the card hurriedly, Robin saw the raised marks of Braille dots. Only three letters had been pressed into the card and Robin studied them. During the last few days she had been trying to memorize the Braille alphabet so that she could learn to read and write it more quickly.

The first letter was ⠎ —an "S", and so was the third. The middle letter was ⠕ —an "O". The message was clear. It read: "SOS." As everyone knew, that was the international call for help.

She wished the day were not so heavy with mist. The

gray murk seemed to press down heavily, blotting out everything that was any distance away, giving the afternoon an eerie, unreal quality. Hurrying again, she went around to the Devery back door. There was no bell, but she banged on the door and called for Flora. The kitchen seemed completely quiet, and curtains hid all the windows. If Flora was in another part of the house, she might never hear because of that bulldozer noise outside. Mrs. Devery was not at home. She had gone off in her car early in the day—on her trip to the ferry and Manhattan. Probably she had not returned, since she expected to be away during the time of the tea party. There was no use consulting Mother, who had her hands full at the moment and would never stop what she was doing unless there seemed to be some urgent need. Whether this note of Stella's was a game, or something important, still remained to be seen.

Robin ran around to the closed front door and rang the bell hard and long. If Flora was in there, she would have to hear that sound. But again all was silent and no one came to the door. Her uneasiness increasing, Robin followed the turn of the veranda, trying to peer into the drawing room, but the long draperies were closed. The house seemed terribly still, as if it held its breath and listened with all its might. Once she thought she heard someone calling from upstairs, but the bulldozer cut in with a dreadful roar and she could not be sure.

She hurried down the steps that led from the veranda to the yard and started again toward the back door. But as she passed the side door that opened to the cellar, it was pushed outward suddenly and a hand reached through the opening and jerked her into the entryway. Robin opened her mouth and yelled with all her might. The door was pulled shut at once and she was closed inside, while outdoor noises drowned out her calls for help. Mr. Lemon had hold of her arm, and he gave her two or three angry shakes.

"Do hush up, little girl," he said. "Nobody can hear you. And you won't be hurt if you'll just keep still. No need to make so much noise."

Robin tried to wrest her arm from his grasp, but he tightened his fingers until the pressure hurt. Upstairs a sudden banging began. Someone was drumming with metal on a radiator, and the sound vibrated throughout the whole house. That was Stella, undoubtedly, but Robin knew the sound would never be heard outside unless someone was near. Not even Mother could hear it, with the din of the party in her ears.

"I'll have to stop that," Mr. Lemon muttered.

To Robin's horror, he opened the door to the dark cellar steps and pushed her through it. "Go down the steps," he ordered. "Go down there and keep still and nobody will hurt you. Hurry now!"

If only she had brought Balmy, Robin thought. She tried to hold back and shouted for Flora, but Mr. Lemon laughed unpleasantly and shook her again.

"Stop that—I warn you!" Mr. Lemon ordered. "Flora's gone. I gave her a fake message and she's gone to the ferry to wait for Mrs. Devery."

A force that was not to be resisted thrust Robin toward the dark stairs and down them a little way. Mr. Lemon let her go, then ran up to the door and closed it tightly. She heard the turning of a key from the other side. The damp, musty emptiness of the cellar seemed to rush up at her, almost as if it were alive and could smother her in dark, silent arms. Robin sat on the steps and clung to the rail, crying softly in her fright.

Her suspicions of Mr. Lemon had been well founded.

He was a wicked person, and now he had everything his own way and could do whatever it was he meant to do. After a while she began to think of Stella, frightened, helpless, and probably locked in her room upstairs. That made the tears stop. If only she could get out of here and up to Stella. But to get out, she would have to leave the comparative safety of the steps and explore that horrid, pitchy blackness below. She knew nothing on earth could make her brave enough for that.

Through the thick stone walls of the old house, the racket of machines sounded faint and far away. The nearer sounds of the tea party were blanketed out. A person shut in down here could scream her head off, and no one outside would hear.

From the door above came again the click of a turning key. Robin squirmed around on the steps. Mr. Lemon peered down at her and nodded his satisfaction.

"That's a good little girl," he said. "Keep still and after a while someone will come to let you out. See, I've brought you company."

From behind him he pulled Stella into the open and thrust her toward the dark opening. Robin had a quick glimpse of her white face, before Stella was on the stairs too and the door above had closed them into darkness, the key turning noisily. Overhead Mr. Lemon's steps sounded as he walked through the house.

"Is it you, Robin?" Stella whispered.

Robin reached out her hand and found the other girl's and they clung to each other. Robin's teeth were chattering and Stella heard them.

"Are you cold?" Stella asked. "I know where there's an old coat on a hook down here."

Through stuttering teeth Robin said she was not cold,

only scared. They couldn't go down there into the darkness and stumble around.

Stella's sudden laughter came as a surprise. "Don't be silly! The cellar isn't dark for me. It's like any other place. Hold onto my arm and I'll lead you. We'll be uncomfortable if we stay here on the stairs."

Robin began to feel less frightened. How strange that in this terrifying place Stella could "see" far better than she could. This girl who might be fearful at a noisy party, or retreat into an imaginary tunnel at the loss of a pin, was the one with courage down here.

Stella moved with confidence and swerved around objects she knew stood in the way of where she wanted to go. Robin followed uncertainly on her heels, one hand in the crook of Stella's arm, their positions reversed from the way they walked in the outside world. Beneath Robin's feet the cement floor felt hard and gritty with the dust of years that had gathered on it.

"Here we are," Stella said. "Old Lemonpuss can't find us, even if he looks. Not unless he brings a light. Watch it—there's an old bed right in our path."

A moment later Robin heard the clang of metal as Stella touched the bed.

"It's not uncomfortable on top of the spring webbing," Stella told her. "This is where I hide when I want to think about something important. Nobody ever comes here but me. Grandmother had this part of the cellar walled off when she put in oil heat. There isn't even a light down here now, I guess. There are better stairs to the other section from across the kitchen. But there's no door through from this part. Take my hand and I'll help you up on the bed."

The metal screeched and groaned as they climbed

onto the springs. There they sat cross-legged, close together for reassurance, suspended well above the floor
and safe enough for the moment. The blackness wasn't
so dreadful, Robin found, with Stella there.

"What do you suppose Mr. Lemon is up to?" she
asked.

"I don't know," Stella said, and went on, her tone
suddenly excited. "Wait till I tell you what happened
this morning! I think Grandmother has been getting
tired of Mr. Lemon and his plans—whatever they are.
While we were eating breakfast, he called me a poor
little blind girl, the way he always does, and Grandmother blew up."

Stella laughed again and the sound was comforting
to hear in the silence of the black cellar.

"She told him never to call me that," Stella went on.
"She said I wasn't a poor little anything. And that I was
a girl—not a blind-girl. She told him I could probably
see better than he could in a lot of ways, and she started
quoting to him out of a book on blindness she's been
reading. After that, she brought out my clay dachshund
and set it down on the table for my mother and Mr.
Lemon to see.

"That's when I told Grandmother how Mr. Lemon
got the lid to the incense burner, and she said that settled matters. She wouldn't give him a penny for his
Cuban project—whatever she meant by that. He started
telling her how well he knew my father in Havana, but
she cut him right off. She said even if he was a relative,
she didn't want anything more to do with him. She told
him he could pack up and leave today. She was going
out and when she came home she expected to find him
gone."

Robin wriggled with satisfaction and the bedsprings

twanged. "Good for your grandmother! What did Mr. Lemon say?"

"He was wild. I could tell by the ugly sound in his voice. He said she would be sorry for treating him this way. He went upstairs and stayed in his room until after she went out. This afternoon he got Flora to go out on an excuse. He told her that Grandmother had phoned from New York and said her car had broken down. She was coming home with a lot of packages and would need help, so Flora must come to the ferry to meet her. Flora didn't know about the quarrel, and he reminded her that he was my relative and said he would look after everything until she got back.

"When she'd gone, he came upstairs to my grandmother's room. After I knew he had lived in Cuba, I began to remember about him and I didn't trust him at all. When I heard him in the hall at the door to Grandmother's room, I told him I'd call your mother on the phone if he went in there. I didn't guess how angry he would get. He made puffing sounds, as though he might explode.

"He made me come up to the third floor and he locked my balcony door and told me to be quiet. Of course I wasn't. I made as much noise as I could, but it didn't do any good because there's so much noise outside and our house is set back so far. I thought of the basket. I broke a pane of glass and took a curtain rod down for a stick. I fished around until I was lucky enough to hook on to the bell cord so I could get your bell to ring. But of course I couldn't put a message into the basket. All I could do was throw one outside when you rang my bell. I hoped it would clear the balcony rail so you'd find it."

"I did," Robin said.

"I know. I could hear you banging on doors and ringing bells and calling. But there wasn't any way to warn
you to watch out for Mr. Lemon."

"How long do you think he'll leave us down here?"
Robin whispered.

"I don't know." Stella's voice was touched with uneasiness.

"I sent you a message in our basket a couple of days
ago," Robin told her. "Why didn't you take it out?
You weren't locked in all that time."

Stella hesitated before answering. "I had to make
up my mind about something first. I was afraid you
might make it hard for me, so I wouldn't look in the
basket."

That was puzzling, but Robin did not prod her further. There were enough immediate problems to worry
about.

The two girls were quiet for what seemed a long
while. As her eyes became accustomed to the gloom,
Robin discovered that the darkness wasn't as pitchy
black as before. A faint grayness seeped into the cellar
from a high place on the outer wall. But before she could
think about investigating, a rustling sound reached her
from not far away.

At once she clutched Stella in fright. "What's that?
What's that rustling?" Robin asked.

Stella spoke calmly. "Don't, you're pinching me. It's
only mice. They won't hurt you."

"Mice!" Robin shrilled, more terrified of mice in the
dark than of anything else she could imagine. She
wrapped her arms frantically around Stella.

This time the other girl sensed her fright and did not
shake her off. "Don't be so scared. Mice are very inter-

esting. Dad got me some white mice for pets when we lived in Havana. I had a rabbit too, and a hamster. As well as a cat and a dog. Mother said our place was like a farm. Dad knew it was hard for me to learn what animals are like. Toy animals don't mean too much. They feel like what they are—wood or plastic, or whatever. So he wanted me to know as much about small animals as I could. Knowing what a cat is like, I can imagine a tiger better—something like a cat, but so many times larger and fiercer. Listen—it's quiet now. You've frightened the mice with all that noise."

Robin unwrapped her arms from about Stella, feeling a little foolish. "But if you've had so many animals for pets, why were you afraid of Balmy when he came barking around you that first time?"

"He was a stranger and I didn't know how big he was, or if he was angry."

Robin could understand how that might be. But as far as she was concerned, these mice were strangers too. It was better to talk than to sit silent and listen for mice, however harmless.

"Have you stopped worrying now?" she asked Stella. "About what?"

"I don't know. You were awfully upset when I left that morning after my visit."

Stella was quiet for so long that Robin thought she did not mean to answer. The other girl changed the subject. "How did the clay head come out? Have you shown it to Mr. Hornfeld?"

"Not yet," Robin said. "I think it's pretty good. I don't know if he'll take me in his class, but at least I'll have something to show him."

"I'm glad," said Stella softly. "I'm awfully glad."

She spoke so fervently that Robin was puzzled. There was something here she did not understand. Stella sounded as though she had fought some battle with herself and found her way through to a decision that had at last satisfied her. Was it possible, Robin wondered, that Stella would have liked to use the dachshund she had made to get into Mr. Hornfeld's class, but had pretended she wasn't interested so that she wouldn't step in ahead of Robin and be chosen instead as a member of the class? If that was true, Robin knew she could not live with herself if she accepted the sacrifice.

"Why did you say you didn't want to make anything else in clay?" she asked.

"I was upset," Stella confessed.

"Would you like to be in Mr. Hornfeld's class?"

"Perhaps," said Stella. "It might be fun."

Robin felt more puzzled than ever.

"You know something?" Stella went on. "I've been thinking over what you said about other people's feelings—about other people hurting inside themselves, the way I do. I suppose I've never thought much about that before. But I'm trying. I'm trying to care about how someone else feels. I think I do care."

There was no telling what she meant, but Robin reached out and squeezed her arm. "That's fine," she said.

Across the cellar the door opened squeakily. Both girls sat so still that not even the springs of the bed creaked beneath their weight. They could see Mr. Lemon silhouetted at the head of the stairs.

"Where are you?" he called, as if he was surprised to find that they had ventured away from the steps.

Neither girl answered, and the darkness must have

blinded him, for he did not see them huddled on the bed.

"Where are you?" he shouted. "Where have you gone?"

Neither girl spoke and he shouted again. "I know you're down there. There's no way to get out. I'm leaving now. I'm going to lock you in, but you'll get out all right when somebody comes home. I want you to give your grandmother a message for me, Stella. Tell her that if she sets the police after me, or if she tries to injure me in any way, I'll tell everything I know, and the lives of men she could help will be in danger. Have you got that?"

Stella spoke up, her voice loud and clear. "I've remembered who you are. I'm going to tell my grandmother."

"How could you remember anything?" he scoffed. "You've never seen me."

"I've heard you," Stella told him. "One time in my father's office in Havana. You aren't a relative at all, are you?"

His laugh was unpleasant. "I lived next door to your Great-aunt Edith for a while. Good-by, little girls. Don't be afraid of the dark."

He slammed the door and locked it, and the girls heard him let himself out the side door.

When he had gone, there was silence again, with only the distant roar of the bulldozer to let them know there was an outside world.

(16)

Secret of the Emerald Star

"DID YOU REALLY know Mr. Lemon in Cuba?" Robin asked when the quiet grew too intense.

"I met him just once. The sound of his voice kept reminding me. As soon as I thought of him as someone I'd met in Havana, I knew who he was. I can't remember his real name, but he worked in my father's office. That is, he worked there until he was fired for something dishonest and Dad wouldn't have him anymore. He must have heard about my father from Edith Devery, and he applied for a job. I met him in Dad's office. My mother left me there while she went shopping, so she never saw him. He came in to speak to my father. Later Dad told us that he'd had to fire him. After that I forgot him. There were worse things to think about."

"Probably the whole thing he told your grandmother about guns for Cuba was dishonest too," Robin said. Released from the need to be silent, she related what had happened that day at teatime before Stella had come downstairs.

"If only Grandmother had let me know," Stella cried. "I'd have remembered him sooner. I'm sure he was after as much of her money as he could get and he was trying to play on her sympathy. He'd never have bought guns nor tried to help my father's friends."

"But what is he up to today?" Robin asked. "Why did he lock us in down here? What was he doing upstairs?"

This puzzled Stella too and she had no answer. "I wish there was some way to get out of here," she said.

Robin stared again at the slight grayness across the cellar. It was high up, under the ceiling and against the outer wall.

"That might be a window up there," she murmured.

Stella was alert at once. "A window? Is it in a place you could get to?"

"I don't know," Robin said. "If I had a long stick, I could prod around and see if I could reach up there."

"I'll get you a stick!" Stella scrambled off the bed and ventured across the cellar.

Robin huddled where she was, listening to her movements. She thought of mice and was sorry she had mentioned a stick. From a distance came the sound of lumber being rattled on the floor. In a few moments Stella returned, dragging with her a thin strip of wood.

"There's a stack of old boards and laths over there that everybody has forgotten about," she said. "This ought to be long enough to reach the ceiling."

Robin fumbled for the wooden strip. It was slightly flexible, but strong, and by tapping the end of it on the floor she could tell that it was very long.

"Go ahead and see what you can do," Stella urged. "Watch out for splinters. I'd try it myself, but I can't tell where the window place is."

Robin took a deep breath and put her feet cautiously on the floor. She didn't dare mention the mice again. Not when Stella was so courageous down here. She could only hope that these mice weren't the affectionate sort who liked human beings and might run over to see what she was doing.

She could not find her way in the dark as well as Stella had, and she bumped into a wooden crate, skinning one shin and knocking over some tall object that felt like a clothes tree. By that time she was close enough to the grayish patch to reach up toward the faint crack of light. She could tell that a board or two had been nailed across an opening up there.

Grit fell on her as she poked, and there were already splinters in her hands, but she kept on trying. The wooden strip was too flexible for hard prying, but by luck the nails in the boards were loose. She pried a bit and heard them squeal as they came free from their holes. When she had tried this in several places, the whole mass of boards suddenly came loose and fell toward her in a shower of dirt and dust, just missing her head as the lot crashed to the floor.

"What has happened?" Stella cried. "Are you hurt?"

"I'm all right," Robin assured her. "It really is a window and it's open now. Can you feel that good fresh air? I guess the glass was broken and somebody boarded it shut."

"Can we get out?" Stella called. "Can we climb up on something and squeeze out?"

The cellar was no longer dark. Outside, the mists had blown away and the sunlight of late afternoon flooded the outdoors and threw shadows upon the cement floor—the long, narrow shadows of iron bars.

Robin hated to tell Stella, but it was necessary. "We couldn't get out even if we climbed up there. The window is big enough to get through, but there are bars across the outside."

Sounds from Catalpa Court came to them more

clearly now. The tea party at the Wards' house was still going on, with all the ladies chattering at once. The noisy bulldozer was still digging away. Robin cupped her hands around her mouth and stood below the window opening. She shouted as loud as she could, calling for help. But the sound seemed to wash back upon her. It echoed loudly through the cellar, making no dent on the noisy court.

"It's no use," she told Stella. "Nobody can hear us."

"Then come back here," Stella said. "We'll have to wait."

In the house upstairs the telephone began to ring and both girls started at the sound. There was no way to answer it. It rang on and on for quite a while and then stopped.

Robin had returned to the haven of the bed and was curled up again beside Stella. They both felt better for the change of air, and Robin at least felt more comfortable with light coming in through the high place near the ceiling. She could understand about Stella's blindness a little better now. Stella didn't miss the light, because she was used to being without it. She didn't think about it as a necessity the way sighted people did when they insisted on pitying the blind.

Stella's words broke softly into her thoughts. "You've made me think about my mother's feelings too, Robin. Sometimes it's as if I wanted to hurt her because something hurts me. But she never gets angry. She knows how much we love each other. And she's wonderful to my grandmother, when most people would get mad."

"I know she is," Robin said. She felt enormously relieved. The memory of Stella turning away from her mother had troubled her more than she had realized. It was good to hear the affection in Stella's voice.

Time went on and the worst of this waiting was that the more time passed the more likely it would be that Mr. Lemon could get away with whatever dishonest thing he might be about. Robin could imagine all sorts of things happening outside. Perhaps Mrs. Devery had been delayed over in Manhattan. Perhaps she had tried to phone to tell them so. Flora wouldn't know, and she might wait endlessly at the ferry on her senseless errand. After a while, night would come. The thought of staying all night in this place was terrifying. No one would know where to look for them, even after Robin was missed.

Stella seemed aware of her worry. She tucked a hand through Robin's arm. "Let's sing," she said. "Dad used to love American western songs. He taught me a lot of them."

Her clear, pure voice took the lead, and Robin's lighter tones followed as they started singing old favorites. "Springtime in the Rockies," "Home on the Range," "Rose of San Antone," and so many others. When they couldn't remember the words, they hummed, and when they couldn't remember the tune, they broke off and tried something else. It was strange how much braver she felt while she was singing, Robin thought.

It took a handful of gravel thrown through the bars of the window to cut off the burst of song. Robin could see a head up there, dark against the sunlight as someone knelt trying to see into the cellar.

"Hey, there!" Julian called. "Are you all right?"

Both girls answered in an excited jumble of words, and Julian had to shout to them to speak one at a time. Robin was silent while Stella called out that they were locked in, and he would have to get them out.

There was a time of waiting, then a sound of breaking glass reached them from the rear of the house as Julian got into the kitchen through a window. Footsteps sounded overhead and in no time the key turned in the cellar door and Julian and Tommy appeared on the steps.

Hand in hand, Robin and Stella crossed the floor and went up the stairs. The house was dim and quiet and the four young people let themselves out the front door and sat on the veranda while explanations were made all around. First about Mr. Lemon, with Stella and Robin taking turns. Then of what Tommy Ward had done to bring about their rescue.

Tommy had not been home when Robin had started her search around the Devery house, but he had seen Mr. Lemon hurrying out of Catalpa Court in a great rush with his suitcase in his hand. Being curious, he had headed right for the Deverys' to see what was up. There seemed to be no one around, but he had found a white card lying on the ground where Robin had dropped it. A card with some dots punched into it. This he had known must be Braille, and he went looking for Julian Hornfeld. When he found the older boy, the two of them had looked up the Braille alphabet in an encyclopedia and deciphered the "SOS" message. All this had taken quite a while. The next move had been to telephone the Devery house. When no one answered, the boys came over and heard the singing down in the cellar. The girls were making so much noise they hadn't heard Julian and Tommy calling until Julian threw a handful of gravel through the window.

The four were still talking and trying to decide what should be done next, when a car turned into the drive

with Mrs. Devery at the wheel and Flora in the front
seat beside her. Both women jumped out of the car the
moment it stopped and ran toward the house.

"Are you all right, Stella?" Mrs. Devery demanded
when she saw the young people on the veranda. She ran
to her granddaughter and put her arms about her.

"That awful Lemon person!" Mrs. Devery cried.
"He played a trick on Flora and sent her on a wild-goose
chase. There was nothing the matter with my car.
Where is he? I want to talk to him!"

"He's gone," Stella said. "He locked Robin and me
in the cellar and went off with his suitcase. And he said
if you tried to set the police after him, he'd tell what he
knew about Father's friends in Cuba."

Mrs. Devery sank into a veranda chair and Flora ran
to get a glass of water. The old lady recovered herself
and waved it away.

"I will not be blackmailed like that," Mrs. Devery
declared. "I don't think he knows anything to tell. This
is terrible and it is my own fault. I never trusted him
fully, but he had so many stories about the old days and
about my son in Cuba that I listened to him. Nevertheless, I was suspicious and so this afternoon I went over
to Manhattan to talk to an attorney who used to take
care of Edith's affairs and had been south several times
to visit her. I told him about this plan of Mr. Lemon's
concerning the guns. And I described the man carefully.
Mr. Scott says the description answers that of a man
who lived in the house next to Edith at one time, and
whose family knew her well. He would have known a
lot about Edith from hearing her talk, but he isn't a relative. Even his own family considered him a ne'er-do-
well. I'm sure he was only playing on my sympathy to

get me to give him money. He thought I was old and foolish and would believe him."

Stella told her own story quickly—of how she remembered Mr. Lemon from her father's office in Cuba. The whole thing began to tie together and add up to the cruel trick Mr. Lemon had tried to play.

Julian remained the calmest person in the midst of this excitement. He pointed out that Mr. Lemon must have locked the girls in the cellar for some purpose that had nothing to do with his original plan.

"Do you suppose he meant to steal something from the house before he ran away?" Julian asked.

Mrs. Devery stared at him in dismay. "It couldn't be money. I never keep money around the house. Though I do have some good pieces of jewelry." Suddenly she sat straight up in her chair, her face white. "There's Stella's emerald star! He knew about that. He knew I had put it in my jewel case for safekeeping. He was in the hall when I took it away from Stella the other night."

Stella gasped and Robin put a reassuring hand on her arm. "Don't worry. Let's wait and see."

Mrs. Devery pushed Flora's ministering hands away and rose from her chair. "I'll go and look at once."

She ran into the house and hurried upstairs. The four young people followed her into the hall and grouped themselves at the foot of the stairs. In a few moments she came out of her room. She descended slowly, leaning heavily on the rail. This time she did not push Flora away, but took her arm when she reached the lower hall. There were tears in her eyes as she looked at Stella. Her iron assurance had faded, and for the moment she was an old and forlorn woman.

"I wish your mother were here," she said to Stella. "I wish I could ask her to tell you. I—I don't know how to."

"You mean Stella's pin is gone?" said Julian gently.

"Yes. He broke open the locked drawer where I kept my jewel case and took everything of value in it. Including Stella's pin. I don't know what to say. I don't know—"

Stella's voice broke in upon her grandmother's faltering words. "It doesn't matter about the pin. It's all right if it's missing."

Mrs. Devery looked at her granddaughter and seemed to pull herself together. "Thank you for your generosity, my dear. But of course it matters. It matters more than any of the other pieces because I took it away from you. I was responsible." She turned toward the telephone in the hall.

"Please!" Stella said. "You don't understand. Mr. Lemon didn't take that pin out of your case. I did."

There was a moment's blank silence while everyone stared at Stella.

"You mean—you can't mean—" her grandmother stumbled over the words, hardly daring to hope.

"I got the key and took the pin out myself," Stella said, sounding defiant. "It was mine. I had a right to it!"

Relief seemed to bring Mrs. Devery to life. "Then the pin is all right. The other things he took aren't so important. Stella, did you put the pin in a safe place where that man wouldn't think to look? You don't suppose—"

"He didn't take it," Stella said firmly. "I took it. I took it and I lost it. It's gone for good. But that's not Mr. Lemon's fault."

"If you lost it, we'll look for it," Mrs. Devery said

firmly. "But now I must call the police." She walked to the telephone in the hall and picked up the receiver.

Stella put out her hand in distress. "Robin—where are you?"

Robin took her hand at once. "I'm right here. I'm sorry about the pin, Stella. If you like, I'll help you look for it."

"We'll all help," Julian said.

Stella held Robin's hand tightly. "No—it's no use. No one can find it. Don't think about it, Robin. It doesn't matter. You made me understand that the star was an idea that *abuela* gave me. I never cared about its value, and I still have the idea. You're my best friend, Robin, and that's more important than anything else. I want you to be happy. I do care about how you feel. So I don't want you to worry about the pin."

Stella was near to crying and before Robin could find words to answer this astonishing outburst, Stella reached for the stair rail and ran upstairs as fast as she could go. They looked after her in surprise.

"What's eating her?" Tommy asked.

Mrs. Devery turned from the phone. "The police are coming over. They're going to send out a description of this man so they can pick him up. I hope your mother will let you come and talk to them, Robin. Both you girls can tell them exactly what happened."

"Of course she'll let me," Robin said. But she was hardly thinking of Mrs. Devery's words. A strange and rather dreadful suspicion was growing in her mind. It had begun to dawn when Stella had said she must be happy. Robin knew she had to get back to her own room where she could figure something out.

"Do you care if I go home first?" she asked Mrs.

Devery. "I—I'm sort of dirty from scrambling around the cellar. I'll come back in a little while."

Mrs. Devery nodded. "Run along. I'll phone when I need you. But first I want to thank all three of you for being so helpful and resourceful."

Julian smiled at her and went outside. By the thoughtful way in which Mrs. Devery looked after him, Robin could tell that she was accepting him at last.

As Robin turned to follow, Tommy stared at her curiously. "You look as though you were seeing ghosts."

She did not answer. This was a time for thinking, for going over every step of a road she knew must lead to disaster.

She ran down the front steps and ducked through the new hole in the hedge. She did not know that Julian had followed her until she was in her own yard.

"Something's wrong," he said. It wasn't a question.

She could only nod helplessly and hurry toward the steps.

"Is there any way I can help?"

"I don't know what to do," Robin said. "I just don't know what to do!" Even as she spoke, she could remember Stella saying the same words. Now she knew what they had meant—knew what they must mean.

Julian did not leave her side, and she sensed his concern for her. He was the sort of person who would worry about someone else's trouble. But there was nothing anyone could do to help. The decision was up to her. First, however, she must be as sure as it was possible to be.

At her own front door Julian stopped her. "Will you show me the clay head of Stella you've done as an entry for Dad's class?" he asked.

She looked at him through swimming eyes. He was trying to be kind, she knew. He was worried about her, and he didn't want to leave her alone. It didn't matter if he saw the head. It was as finished as it would ever be.

"All right, I'll let you see it," she said, and they went into the house.

The tea party was coming to an end, and the two hurried past the living room door and ran upstairs before any grown-ups could call to them. Robin opened the door of her room and turned at once to the clay head. It stood on the big table that had been brought inside and was taking up so much space. There were no longer any damp cloths over the clay, since it was almost dry.

Julian gave a long, low whistle and went straight to the head. Robin turned her back and walked out on the balcony. She leaned on the rail and stared into a green world of tree branches and singing birds. One by one she went over the steps in her mind. One by one she set up the chain of evidence that could lead only in one direction. When she had gone all the way through the steps twice, she knew what had to be done. She returned to her room where Julian was studying the head.

"This is good," he said. "You've caught that look Stella gets on her face sometimes. Sort of sad and unsure and expectant—all at once. There is more you need to know about how to work, but when Dad sees this, he'll be sure to take you into his class."

Robin blinked her eyes hard, trying to gain some measure of comfort from his words. "Your father makes it a rule that each student has to bring a piece of work with him, doesn't he?"

"That's right. Something to use as a measuring stick. He wouldn't take you otherwise."

"It will be a long time before I can do anything else as good as this," she said, touching the head lightly. "I think I did it on pure inspiration. It came out of the way I feel about Stella. I don't think I could do it again because I don't really know how. That's why I wanted so much to be in your father's class. So I could learn."

"You'll be there," Julian said, completely assured.

"No," said Robin, "I won't be."

Before he could guess what she meant to do, before he could move to stop her, she picked up the small bronze elephant from her dresser. The bronze was heavy and she smashed it down on the head as hard as she could. The dry, brittle clay shattered in all directions. She was aware of the clatter of small pieces skittering across the floor and of Julian staring at her in horror, as if he thought she had taken complete leave of her senses. The head was broken to bits and done with forever.

Robin swallowed hard and knelt on the floor to fumble among the pieces. She found what she searched for almost at once and held it up for Julian to see.

"Stella's emerald star," she said, and knelt there, staring at the ugly bits of broken clay that had once been something so beautiful. In that instant it came to her that there might have been some other way, some less drastic way. If only she had waited, if she had consulted Julian! Yet she could not be wholly sorry. She had done what she had felt it was right to do, no matter how difficult.

There was a dawning of understanding in Julian's eyes, but if he thought she had been foolish, he did not say so. He took the star pin from her and examined it thoughtfully. "How did you know?" he asked.

She gave him the steps one by one, from the moment

when Mrs. Devery had found the pin on Stella's pajamas and told her she could not keep it anymore. Stella
had been furious and resentful. She had been frightened
too, because she needed the pin to keep her out of that
tunnel.

The next morning when Robin awakened, Stella had
been out of the room. When she returned, she had
seemed keyed up about something. She must have had
the pin in her hand then, having taken it out of her
grandmother's case. Robin had gone off for her turn in
the bathroom. Stella, seeking for a safe place to hide the
pin, and not knowing that Robin had turned the card
table around, must have gone to the clay head she
thought was hers. In her anger and haste she must not
have checked the head carefully with her fingers. Perhaps she had been so sure she had sought only one unfinished eye socket. It made a perfect temporary place
for hiding the pin. When she broke up the clay later she
could retrieve it. So she had pressed the pin deep into
the eye hollow and smoothed the rough spot over.

Not until later when the girls had carried their work
downstairs must Stella have realized that she had buried
the emerald star in an eye socket of the wrong head.
Robin remembered very well how frantically Stella had
run her hands over Robin's piece. Robin had stopped
her. She had told her that the head was coming right at
last and she wasn't going to have it spoiled.

Julian sighed unhappily. "She should have told you
then."

"I know why she didn't. She knew I would have to
spoil my work trying to dig the pin out, and she knew
how much I wanted to be in your father's class. Afterward she must have felt terrible. I remember the way

she broke up that head she was doing of Mr. Lemon and rolled the clay into long snakes. She hung them around her neck and went off to her cellar hiding place to think everything over. Probably she went through every bit of that clay again, to make sure she wasn't wrong and the pin might still be found."

"And when she came back, she still didn't tell you," Julian said. "That was foolish, but it was pretty generous and brave of her too."

Robin nodded. "I know. As soon as I started putting together the things she had said and done, I knew I had to get the pin back for her."

Robin took the emerald star from Julian's hand and held it for a moment, trying to sense the way it felt to Stella. She could make out the points and the bumps that were the stones set into each prong. The gold backing felt smooth and warm from Julian's hand and her finger pricked itself on the point of the catch. She knew what she would do with it.

She wrapped it carefully in a piece of tissue paper and went out on the balcony. She put the small packet in the waiting basket and sent it across to the other balcony. Over there a bell sounded as she jerked the nylon cord.

Stella had apparently recovered the key to her balcony door, for as Robin and Julian watched, she came outside and felt for the basket on its cord. In a moment she held the small wad of tissue in her fingers and was unwrapping it, clearly excited. Robin heard her cry of delight as she found the pin.

"Robin, are you there?" Stella called out anxiously.

"I'm here," Robin said. "Don't worry. I can make another clay head."

"Thank you, Robin!" Stella cried. "I *do* thank you!"

Robin was crying a little, but she had to smile too as she watched Stella disappear indoors. "I think she's going to like Catalpa Court," she said to Julian.

"Are you going to try another clay head?" Julian asked.

"I have to try, don't I?" Robin said. "That's the only way I can learn. But I don't think I can do another right away as good as that. And your father won't accept anything second-rate."

"Dad says second-rate is when we don't try for the best that's in us," Julian said. "But maybe you'd better not do another head of Stella right away. You might keep thinking of the one you'd done and that would make you stiffen up. I know a model who's worth your trying."

Robin regarded him hopefully. "You do?"

"Come here," he said and drew her into the room. He took her by the shoulders, turning her to face the mirror over her dresser. "There you are! You couldn't go wrong with that girl for a model."

She sensed the admiration in his words and looked at her own reflection wonderingly. The girl in the mirror had a mist in her eyes and a tear had made a streak down one cheek. But she was smiling too, and she didn't look one bit like the sort of girl who would give up trying.

"I'll go to work right away," she promised Julian. "There are only a few days left, but at least this model will be handy for posing."

He smiled at her approvingly.

Downstairs the telephone rang and a moment later Mother's voice called up the stairs, sounding puzzled. "Robin! Mrs. Devery is on the phone and she says you are wanted by the police! Do come down here and tell me what this is all about."

Robin and Julian looked at each other and burst out laughing. She could even feel sorry for Mr. Lemon now, since he was a foolish, rather stupid man who would have a penalty to pay for his lawbreaking efforts.

Together Robin and Julian went downstairs to reassure her mother. Robin's tears were gone and hope had started up again. The "lion" was still there in the clay and she was eager to try again and see if she could get it out. She knew that even if she didn't have something for Mr. Hornfeld's class this time, she would want to keep trying. And when she was good enough, the day would come. In the meantime it was the shaping of the clay that mattered, the creating out of herself. Her fingers had that tingly feeling again. She would hurry to Mrs. Devery's and get back home as quickly as she could to start in all over again.

About This Book

Several of my books for young people have been set in foreign countries that I visited in order to gather background material for stories. When I do not go on such a trip, I look for some engrossing subject or place near at hand that I may want to write about.

For some time, articles and books written by blind people had fascinated me, and I finally decided that in my next story I would use a character who was blind. I did not want to treat the subject of blindness in an old-fashioned and sentimental way. The research I had been doing had opened a completely different approach. I began to realize that a blind person, like the rest of us, wants to be treated like anyone else and judged on his own merits without any overemphasis on blindness.

Before long the character of Stella began to present itself in my imagination. I could see her as a very real twelve-year-old with worthwhile qualities and also a good portion of faults, just as anyone else has. I felt that she would be worth knowing in her own right and that she and my heroine, Robin, could help each other a great deal.

When I had done more reading on the subject of blindness, I visited a school in Manhattan where blind

231

children attend classes along with those who can see—
which is the modern approach. I was able to spend an
entire day in a home room where blind students came
between classes and where they studied Braille. I talked
to each young person individually and found that there
was a great difference in the attitude each one had to
this handicap. But in every case the resentment toward
pity emerged. I began to see that it is not the blind who
think about their blindness all the time, but rather the
sighted person who is with them. We are apt to place a
wall of misunderstanding between ourselves and the
blind person which makes it difficult to become friends.
I felt that I wanted to write a story that would help to
tear down that wall.

Jamie Sue Brown, to whom this book is dedicated,
taught me a great deal during that visit to her school.
Her courage and good humor, her interest in all that
was going on about her, impressed me at once. She had
not allowed blindness to shut her away. After school she
invited me to her home, and I was able to walk with her
and learn the proper way to assist a blind person on the
street. She showed me how confidently and capably she
could move about, how well she could use the four good
senses that were hers. She showed me her room, her
record player, radio, and television set, all of which she
enjoys. I learned how she keeps her clothes in order by
herself, and how she arranges her dresser so that everything can easily be found.

That evening I went home full of the ideas I wanted
to set down in a book—points I could make that might
help the sighted to understand the blind, and perhaps
the other way around too.

This time I chose as a background the type of old

neighborhood that exists on Staten Island, where I now live, and I made up the place called Catalpa Court. Since such neighborhoods have people of different religions and races living together in friendly fashion, I made my hero a Jewish boy, Stella a Catholic, and Robin a Protestant.

Of all the characters I have written about, I believe these are the ones I love best. Certainly they were the hardest to part with when I came to the end of the story. I am glad that I have only to open the book to meet them again and renew my own friendship with them.